"I've seen Simone Biles grow as a person and gymnast over the past several years, and what is perhaps most impressive of all is Simone's genuine, kind-hearted spirit and love of life. As one of her biggest fans, I am excited about what the undoubtedly bright future has in store for this fantastic and admirable young woman. As you read the pages of *Courage to Soar*, you will delight in getting to know this Olympic champion who was allowed to be a child and has grown up in a loving family that still plays a huge part in balancing her life. She is everything you would hope for in a champion—humble, kind, genuine, and an overall amazing human being."

—DOMINIQUE MOCEANU, youngest Olympic US gold medalist in gymnastics history (age 14) and New York Times bestselling author of Off Balance

"Simone's narrative outlines a great success story for all ages. In *Courage to Soar*, you will learn firsthand how Simone was able to combine her great natural talent with dedication, perseverance, and, yes, sometimes small sacrifices, in order to reach her goal. I truly enjoyed being part of her journey to world fame!"

—MARTHA KAROLYI, US National Team coordinator, 2000 to 2016, including the Olympics

"Simone Biles became America's sweetheart this summer in Rio, but her story is what will make people fall in love with her forever. Filled with strength, courage, and inspiration, *Courage to Soar* is truly a remarkable story about an amazing athlete and person. Not only did I enjoy the journey Simone takes you on, but I continuously felt inspired through each chapter."

—NASTIA LIUKIN, five-time Olympic medalist, motivational speaker, broadcaster

COURAGE TO
SOAR

A BODY IN MOTION, A LIFE IN BALANCE

SIMONE BILES

WITH MICHELLE BURFORD

ZONDERVAN®

ZONDERVAN

Courage to Soar
Copyright © 2016 by Simone Biles

This title is also available as a Zondervan ebook.

This title is also available as a Zondervan audio edition.

Requests for information should be addressed to:
Zondervan, *3900 Sparks Drive SE, Grand Rapids, Michigan 49546*

ISBN 978–0–310–75966–9

Cover design: Ron Huizinga
Interior design: Denise Froehlich

Printed in the United States of America

16 17 18 19 20 21 22 23 24 25 /DHV/ 20 19 18 17 16 15 14 13 12 11 10 9 8 7 6 5 4 3 2 1

To Mom and Dad:
Your love keeps me grounded yet gives me
the courage to soar toward my dreams.

TABLE OF CONTENTS

The Power of a
Dream

Foreword by Mary Lou Retton

The first time I met Simone Biles, I knew she was special. She was an outrageously talented twelve-year-old dynamo, and I was handing her a gold medal at the Mary Lou Retton Invitational meet in Houston. As she gave that now famous smile and thanked me, I immediately noticed she possessed a unique combination of skill and character: an incredible God-gifted athleticism and explosive power on the mat, a commitment to doing the hard work, and, most important of all, the grace, belief, and joy in gymnastics that would take her all the way. It was only a matter of time before the world learned just how high Simone could fly.

Even before the 2016 Olympics, Simone had already amassed a total of fourteen World medals, ten of them gold, the most ever won by an American female gymnast. She'd garnered three consecutive World Championship titles—the only woman to win three in a row—and claimed her fourth straight US National title. In Rio, on the world's biggest stage, she quickly added to that medal count when the American women took gold in the team competition. Then, in the all-around final, Simone continued her historic bid, posting huge scores on vault, uneven bars, and beam. But this was the Olympics, and Russia's Aliya Mustafina and Simone's own teammate Aly Raisman were on her heels. In the final rotation, Simone was the last to take the floor.

Watching her, my mind flashed back to my own make-or-break Olympic moment in Los Angeles in 1984, when all that stood between me and the all-around gold medal was a flawless routine. In my case, the last rotation was vault, and my coach, Bela Karolyi, was on the sidelines yelling, "You can do it, Panda! Never better!" Hearing my nickname, and feeling the full weight of everyone's hopes, I focused. Somehow, I knew I would do the vault of my life that day. It didn't matter that an American gymnast had never won the Olympic all-around. I would be excellent, because I believed I could be.

Now, all these years later in Rio, as Simone saluted the judges and stepped onto the mat, something about the way she held her shoulders, loose yet determined, told me that she, too, believed. I thought, *She's got this.* The crowd hushed. The music rose. And Simone took off, tumbling, spinning, and soaring her way into the record books. Her routine was impeccable. She didn't just win—she dominated. I may have been the first American gymnast to earn all-around Olympic gold, and I'm proud of that, but I'm even more proud that I'm now part of a special sorority that includes Carly Patterson in 2004, Nastia Liukin in 2008, Gabby Douglas in 2012, and in 2016, Simone Biles.

After Simone's all-around win, Nastia Liukin, an NBC Olympic commentator, declared, "Simone Biles is the best we've seen." And US team captain Aly Raisman, who took silver in the Olympic all-around, joked that second place was the first slot available to the rest of the field, because Simone was in a class of her own. Over the course of the two-week competition, Simone would earn five medals in all—two more golds in the event finals for vault and floor, and a bronze for the balance beam. She became the first American woman ever to win the vault title, and the only one to take home four gold medals in a single Olympic year.

Everyone now knows what I sensed in Simone back in 2009—that she is one of the greatest athletes of all time. In Rio, she remained steady and even lighthearted in the midst of a media storm of expectations. She resisted the hype. She simply went into the arena and did her job, enjoying every moment without allowing the weight of what she'd set out to accomplish to crush her. She understood that whatever happened, as long as she did her best out there, she would get up the next morning, still smiling. This is what I've come to admire most about Simone—her ability to stay humble, shake off setbacks, cheer wholeheartedly for her teammates, and stand in her own true light.

Like all of us, Simone has faced her share of adversity. As her story here will reveal, she has had her dark days, her moments of despair. But she has emerged from her trials and sacrifices stronger and more determined to make them count. And along the way, she has helped to transform gymnastics, pushing its athleticism to new heights. When I went to the Los Angeles Olympics in 1984, female gymnasts were expected to be cute little pixies; slender, graceful butterflies. I was never that. I was solid and muscular, a born tumbler, exploding off the apparatus with force. Mine was the kind of athletic power more often associated with male gymnasts than female. Today, that very style is Simone's strength. Combined with her skill and artistry, her level of difficulty and technical mastery are nearly unbeatable, which may be why Simone hasn't lost an all-around meet since 2013. Thanks to Simone and her generation of competitors—and to the oversight of the now legendary USAG women's coordinator Martha Karolyi (who's been described as her husband Bela's "engine")—female gymnasts are no longer asked to be demure little girls as they perform what may well be the hardest and most dangerous maneuvers in all of sports. With Simone at the forefront, American women gymnasts have embraced and now fully express their formidable athletic power.

When I give motivational talks to young people, I tell them that if they truly believe in themselves, and are willing put in the effort, they can achieve anything. Simone is living proof of that. Back when I was coming up, my only role models were gymnasts on the other side of the globe. Now, American girls with Olympic-sized dreams don't have to look any farther than home to find the best in the sport. But it's important for them to understand that every victory they witness is the pinnacle of a lifetime of hard work and a willingness to confront life's obstacles. Simone was able to stand on the Olympic medal podium, not once but five times, because through all her struggles, doubts, and personal sacrifices, she never gave up. Simone *believed* she could be excellent. You'll come away from her inspiring story knowing that you can be too.

CHAPTER 1

Decision Day

*"You will not always be strong, but
you can always be brave."*

—BEAU TAPLIN, WRITER

My eyes stayed glued to the Jumbotron high above the arena. It was Day 2 of the 2011 Visa National Championships in St. Paul, Minnesota, and I was waiting to see if I'd made the USA Gymnastics (USAG) women's artistic junior team. My heart was pounding so hard that I thought everyone could hear it. After competing against the best of the best in my sport, had I actually made the cut?

We all knew the rules: Only the most qualified gymnasts would make the team. And as always, USAG coordinator Martha Karolyi would have the final say on which gymnasts, and how many, would represent our country. For years, I'd dreamed of being one of those powerful girls in their shimmering leotards, flying through air, sticking the landing every time. I'd imagined having medals around my neck, chalk dust on my legs, and a bright smile on my face. More than anything in the world, I wanted to be chosen for the team.

My parents, Ron and Nellie, have always taught me that the first step to making dreams real is to ask for God's guidance. Did I mention that I'd been doing that all year? In church every Sunday, with my younger sister, Adria, at my side, I'd kneel with my eyes tightly shut and pray for my family and my teammates. I'd then visualize making the national team, imagining it like a movie. That was my prayer, and I believed God was with me on this. After all, he'd given me not just my love of gymnastics, but also the courage to fly high above the arena floor. But had I done enough? As I held my breath and gazed up at the screen, all I could do was hope.

At the time, I was fourteen and small for my age. A four-feet-eight-inch ball of nonstop energy, I liked to say I was four feet nine just so I could feel taller. But I was also strong. I'd been born with the kind of biceps and muscled calves that, back in third grade, had earned me the nickname *swoldger*—a cross between *swollen* and *soldier*. Some girls might have been offended by that, and at first, I did think it was kind of mean. But after a while, I embraced it. I was like, *Yeah, I'm stronger than half of the boys in my class, so don't mess with me.* It helped that I was starting to rack up some wins in gymnastics meets, where most of my teammates had muscles too.

By the time I got to Nationals, I'd been training at Bannon's Gymnastix in Houston, Texas, since I was six. Believe it or not, that's actually pretty late for an elite gymnast. Most girls are flipping and tumbling in Mommy and Me classes before they're three, so in a way, I'd been playing catch-up. But if there's one thing everyone knows about me, it's that I love a challenge.

Maybe because I was always so much smaller than everyone around me, I had this fierce drive to prove myself. So if someone told me to do five push-ups, I'd do ten. If someone tried to tell me I couldn't perform a skill (except maybe on bars, but we'll get to that later), it only made me want to do that skill flawlessly.

That didn't mean I was reckless. Competitive gymnastics can be a dangerous sport, and I understood just how important it was to be well-prepared. In competition, we always performed the skills we'd practiced and mastered in the gym, because as any gymnast can tell you, there's a fine line between being courageous and ending up with a major injury.

At the Visa National Championships, I'd had to walk that line. Martha Karolyi had sent word through my coach, Aimee Boorman, that she wanted to see me perform the Amanar, aka the two-and-a-half twist, which includes a round-off back handspring entry and a two-and-a-half twist on the layout. In other words, it's one of the hardest vaults in the world—and I had never performed it in competition.

"Aimee, I'm not ready!" I said, hyperventilating. "I haven't practiced the two-and-a-half enough. It's not safe."

"Simone, you're the one who has to go out there and do the vault," she told me calmly. "So whatever you decide, I'll support you."

In the end, I stuck with my planned back handspring double-twisting Yurchenko, a vault I knew I could pull off. But my execution that day wasn't the greatest. I'd blasted off the vault with too much power, which caused me to lose control and make an obvious hop on the landing. Long story short, I barely squeaked out a tie for seventh on the vault.

Then again, given that this was my first season as an elite junior gymnast, I'd medaled more than I thought I would. To my surprise, I'd even finished first in some events at earlier meets. But as I went up against the girls I admired—stars like Lexie Priessman, Katelyn Ohashi, Madison Desch, and Amelia Hundley—I was intimidated by how good they were. There was something else too: I thought that if I went out and beat these girls, they wouldn't like me. And more than anything, I wanted these girls to see me as one of them. At Nationals, this lack of confidence had messed with my head.

Now, as I watched the mega screen where the roster of names would appear, I felt, deep down, that I could've done better. Maybe if I'd trained more, spent longer hours practicing in the gym, mastered more challenging skills—like the Amanar—I might be feeling less scared.

A roar went up in the arena as the name of the highest scoring junior gymnast lit the screen. Katelyn Ohashi. No surprise there. Katelyn had killed it on all her routines. I cheered for her loudly.

One by one, the rest of the names appeared on the

overhead screen. Number two, Kyla Ross. Number three, Sarah Finnegan. Number four, Lexie Priessman. I held my breath, wishing with everything in me that my name would be next. Number ten. Number eleven. Number twelve. Then came the final girl—Madison Desch, number thirteen. One row below the list of winners, at number fourteen, I saw my own name. I'd missed making the junior national team by one spot. *One.*

I kept a smile plastered on my face as an announcer called each new team member to the stage. The rest of us stood on the sidelines as the chosen ones laughed and high-fived and hugged each other. As devastated as I felt, I was still happy for the other girls; they'd worked hard to make it this far. Still, I had to swallow my own disappointment as I watched photographers snap pictures that would later appear in *USA Gymnastics* magazine, *Sports Illustrated, Time for Kids.* All the glossies I'd pored over in my bedroom at home, admiring the gymnasts who'd reached the top of the sport.

Tears were bubbling up inside me, but I refused to let the other girls or the coaches see me cry. I kept telling myself I'd done my best, trying to drown out the little voice in my head that whispered, *But did you really? Couldn't you have worked a little harder? Why didn't you do more?* The truth is that my heart was breaking. I had come to Nationals with a goal of making the 2011 team, and it didn't happen. I simply hadn't been good enough.

That's how my journey as an elite gymnast began—with a defeat that put an ache in my heart and doubts in my mind. As much as my family and coaches had cheered me on through hours and hours of training, through wobbles and missteps, through bumps and bruises, I was always secretly afraid that I'd let them and myself down.

Maybe it's good we don't know what will happen next in our stories, because if we did, we might not turn the page. Or we might skip ahead and never experience the good that comes out of the hard moment we're living through.

I thought my failure at the 2011 Nationals was an ending, but it was really a beginning—a turning point on a journey I still can't believe I'm taking. No one is more surprised than I am that the little girl with the big muscles ended up on a path from foster care to an Olympic stadium in Rio de Janeiro, Brazil. Some might call that destiny. I call it a blessing, a gift from God, and a miracle.

CHAPTER 2

Spring

"Love recognizes no barriers. It jumps hurdles, leaps fences, penetrates walls to arrive at its destination full of hope."

—Maya Angelou, poet and author

I wasn't born a Texas girl. In fact, before I called my parents Momma and Poppa Biles, I knew them as Grandma and Grandpa. Actually, I first called them "Hamma" and "Hampaw" because I was only three years old and couldn't enunciate my *g*s.

Hampaw was a tall, medium-brown man with a salt-and-pepper goatee, and Hamma was a short, light-brown woman with soft, curly hair. They both had kind eyes. Before I moved to Texas, they'd come to visit our house in Columbus, Ohio, which was where I lived back then. She was a regional nurse who traveled a lot for her job, and he was a retired Air Force sergeant who now worked as an air traffic assistant with the Federal Aviation Administration in Houston. A few years later, they became the only real parents I've ever known—the ones who have raised and guided me, and loved me every day of my life.

I'll rewind a bit. The woman who gave birth to me in Columbus, Ohio, was Poppa Biles' daughter from a previous marriage. Her name was Shanon, and she'd mostly grown up with her mother in Columbus. Life ended up being a little rocky for Shanon, because as she grew older, she got caught up in drinking and drugs. When I came along on March 14, 1997, my older sister, Ashley, had just turned seven and my brother, Tevin, was almost three. Two years later, on January 27, 1999, my little sister Adria was born. By then, our life with Shanon had started to become difficult.

I don't recall much about living with Shanon, but for some weird reason I do remember playing with a cat. I don't think it was our cat. Maybe it belonged to a neighbor or maybe it was just a stray. Anyway, this cat was always being fed—and at the time, we were hungry at lot, so I was always kind of mad at this cat. Another time, we were having breakfast at our uncle Danny's house. I can still see us pouring dry cereal into our bowls and then putting water on it because we didn't have any milk. It's funny how both of my earliest memories have to do with food.

That was the same year that neighbors called social

services and said we were being neglected, because they saw the four of us were often alone, little kids playing out in the street with no supervision. Soon after that, child protective services came to take my brother, sisters, and me away from Shanon. The social worker rounded us up and sat us down on the steps in front of Shanon's house.

"We're placing you kids in foster care," she said, carefully watching our faces. "It's just for a little while, so Shanon can try to get better."

Most people might think that at age three I was too young to know what it meant to be placed into foster care, but the truth is I understood everything. When the social worker piled the four of us into her car, I knew exactly what was going on. We were going to live with a new family, and we didn't know if we'd like it there. I think we were all a little scared, because none of us said a word during the car ride. Yet as clearly as I remember the heavy silence in the backseat of that car, with Ashley holding four-month-old Adria on her lap, the rest of my foster care memories are fuzzy images.

One memory I do recall is Tevin pushing Ashley and me on a swing in our foster family's backyard. I used to imitate my brother by swinging high and doing backflips off that play set, soaring through the air. "Simone, you can fly! You can fly!" Tevin would yell, running to where I'd landed in a tumble on the grass. My brother was two years older, but I could do all the tricks he could.

There was also a trampoline in the yard, but the foster kids weren't allowed to jump on it in case we got injured. I'd watch my foster parents' biological children, who were older than us, flipping and somersaulting and having so much fun on that trampoline, and I wanted so badly to join them. It wasn't that my foster parents didn't want us to have fun; they were doing their best to keep us safe, especially me since I was so small. But I just knew I could do the moves the older kids did—I was already a fearless little tomboy. I had these miniature six-pack abs and lightning-fast legs. I just couldn't sit still. I was always running and jumping, cartwheeling and somersaulting.

Back then, Tevin was my rock, my protector. I used to watch him and pretty much do whatever he did. I always looked around to make sure I could see him nearby, because he was our little soldier; he made me feel safe. At night, I'd sneak across the hall into the boys' room, where I'd curl up and sleep next to Tevin. I knew our foster mother would gently scold me in the morning, but I just kept doing it. I guess I've always been stubborn. You could say it's my best and worst quality. Later, when I got into gymnastics, that stubbornness was mostly a good thing.

In foster care, Ashley and Tevin missed Shanon a lot, but I didn't really mind our new situation. We ate breakfast every morning and dinner every night, and we even went camping with our foster family once or twice. We always had lots of other kids to play with and even a furry little Beagle named Teddy. And our foster parents, Miss Doris and Mr. Leo, were nice to us. I remember one time I wanted a lollipop from the cookie jar on the counter. I was just a little thing, but somehow I managed to get myself up onto that counter, where Miss Doris found me trying to pry open the cookie jar.

"Now how on earth did you get up there!" she said as she lifted me down to the floor. "Simone, don't ever climb up here again! You could hurt yourself!" Her voice was stern, but really, she was a softie. After setting me down to the floor, she handed me the lollipop.

We'd been in foster care for just a few months when my grandfather appeared on Miss Doris and Mr. Leo's doorstep. "Grandpa's here!" Tevin whispered to me as he came into the living room. Our social worker, a warm-hearted African-American woman, was next to Grandpa. She explained we'd be traveling back to Texas with our grandfather the next day. We'd be going on a plane—my first airplane ride—and our grandparents would take care of us while Shanon tried to get better in an outpatient rehab program.

I learned later that the social worker had called our grandfather to tell him we'd been taken into foster care. When he heard that, he immediately started making calls and talking to lawyers and doing whatever he had to do to arrange for the four of us to move in with him and my grandma. "Nellie," he'd said to my grandma, "I want to bring the children here to live with us until Shanon gets herself together. I can't stand the thought of those kids being scattered to strangers." Of course, I didn't know any of this was happening until the day he came to pick us up.

Can you imagine suddenly taking in four children? For my grandma, that wasn't an easy decision, because she didn't know us very well back then. My grandpa had visited us in Ohio often, but Grandma Nellie had been with him only a few of those times. She usually stayed at home with their two sons, Ron II and Adam. Ron was sixteen and a high school sophomore; Adam was fourteen and a freshman. My grandparents were almost done raising their boys, and now here we were, four young children who needed the kind of attention and care that Grandma Nellie thought she was about to retire from.

"Okay, Ron," she said to my grandpa. "Let me pray on this."

She needed time to wrap her mind around the idea of doubling the size of her family. She also had to make peace with the fact that her dreams of traveling the world would have to be put on hold. Busy as she was with her nursing career, she also worried about whether she could truly give us the care we needed, especially after the disruption we'd experienced with Shanon. Grandma figured that Adria and I would be easy enough, but Ashley and Tevin had much stronger memories of life with Shanon. Understandably, they were very attached to her.

That week, during a lunch break at work, my grandma ended up talking to a woman she'd never met. This woman told her a story about adopting a child with extreme physical and emotional needs. At first, the woman had resisted taking responsibility for this child because she didn't think she was strong enough for the task. But she finally decided to do what God had asked of her. She was so glad that she had, because the child was doing well and had brought such joy to her life. "That child has been God's gift to me," she told my grandma. "I can't imagine what my life would be like if I'd passed up this great blessing."

Here was this complete stranger pouring out her heart, and my grandma was getting the message loud and clear. "You know, honey, the Lord doesn't make any mistakes," the woman continued. "And he never gives you more than you can handle." She then patted my grandma on the shoulder and left.

As Grandma was driving home that night, tears flowed down her cheeks. She understood that God was asking her to open her heart to us, and he'd sent that woman as a guardian angel to tell her everything would be okay. God himself was placing us in her care. That's when she knew we were going to live with her and Grandpa, because we were family, and you never turn your back on family. More than that, you never turn your back on God.

Shanon wanted to see us before we left for Texas, so we met up with her at the child protective services office in Columbus. Ashley and Tevin burst into tears when they saw her walking toward us with the social worker at her side. My sister and brother ended up sniffling all the way to Houston because they wanted to go back home. Adria and I didn't cry. My grandpa says Adria slept in Ashley's arms for most of the plane ride, while I was smiling so hard that he put his forehead to mine and teased, "Oh no, little miss Simone, you're not going to steal my heart."

My grandpa was actually the one who had suggested the name Simone for me. He'd liked the sound of it ever since he was a teenager listening to Nina Simone records in the housing projects in Cleveland. I've always loved knowing that he was the one who named me. It's like, right from the start, he was watching over me.

The five of us landed in Houston on a warm afternoon in March 2000. My grandma met us at the airport, and from there we drove twenty-five miles north to a suburb called Spring. When we pulled into the driveway, I bounded out of the car and ran into the house, the beads in my box braids swinging around my face. I'd never seen a house as beautiful as Grandma and Grandpa's home, with its gleaming floors, big eat-in kitchen, and a wide stairway up to the second floor. At the top of the stairs were the two bedrooms where the four of us would sleep. My room was furnished with a crib for Adria and a bunk bed for Ashley and me. Tevin would be in a room with Adam.

Grandma's friends had thrown her a shower at work, because they knew that with four young kids moving in, she might need some help getting up to speed. They gave her a crib and lots of diapers and baby bottles for Adria; Barbie dolls and clothes for me; and cool stuff like backpacks and Razor scooters for Ashley and Tevin. One friend even gave her the bunk bed that Ashley and I would sleep on—I immediately started swinging and somersaulting from the wooden slats under the top bunk and nearly destroyed several of them! In the closet and chest of drawers were more clothes and shoes, and on the shelves were Junie B. Jones storybooks and a Cinderella collection that, if you put the books together in the right order, created a picture of a castle across the bindings. I think we felt as if we were in a fairy tale of our own, because everywhere we looked there were shiny new things that our grandparents thought we'd need for life in Spring.

I climbed up onto a chair beside the window of the girls' room as my grandma was pointing out our beds. And guess what I spotted in the backyard? *A trampoline*!

"Hamma! Hamma! Can I play on that?" I asked, hopping down off the chair and pointing at the window excitedly.

My grandma looked confused, but Adam, standing at the doorway, knew what I was talking about. "The trampoline?" he said. "Sure! Want to go jump on it right now?"

I just stood there for a second, staring at Adam with my eyes wide and my mouth hanging open. And then I ran back downstairs as quickly as my tiny legs would carry me, through the living room and the kitchen, and I didn't stop till I was in the yard, climbing up onto that trampoline. For what seemed like hours, I bounced and twirled and flipped and somersaulted, my beaded braids flying up into the sky again and again, as if they could touch heaven.

The first thing my grandma did when I came back inside was to put me between her knees to comb out my tangled hair. She undid each braid and removed every bead, then washed and combed and brushed. When she was done, I felt like a brand-new princess with my hair neatly parted down the center and redone in two braids. I loved the feel of my grandma's hands in my hair. I loved the look of concentration on her face as she worked. I just sat there daydreaming about this new life I was entering, my elbows resting on my grandma's knees. I was happy; I knew because the knots I usually felt in my tummy were gone.

As the oldest, Ashley helped out with Adria and me, getting us dressed, playing with us, and settling us down to sleep at night. I still didn't like sleeping alone, and neither did Adria, so most nights I would climb into my baby sister's crib and drift off next to her. My grandma was always surprised to find us together in the same bed come morning. She thought Ashley was letting down the side of Adria's crib, until one day she walked in and saw me with one leg slung over the top of the rail, hoisting myself over.

Back then, I had Adria under my complete control, taking her everywhere in the house and yard with me. I seemed to believe that I was in charge of her, and even with our grandparents now looking out for us, I would always hold her hand and wipe her face if she was crying, and I'm sure I also told her what to do and how to do it. Oh, I was a bossy little thing, even though I couldn't pronounce my gs properly! My big-sister protectiveness didn't change right away. Actually, it still hasn't changed. Even now, I watch out for Adria.

It wasn't long before Adria became super attached to our grandparents. It used to be that she'd fuss if she didn't see me nearby. After a while, I could come and go without her noticing, but she'd burst into tears whenever Grandma went into the next room. In the mornings when Ashley and Tevin got dropped off at school and us younger ones got dropped off at day care, my baby sister would cry inconsolably. And at dinner each night, Adria would wriggle her way out of her high chair, toddle over to Grandma, climb into her lap, and finish her plate there. Grandma allowed my sister to stick to her like glue because she knew Adria needed that security.

Maybe I needed security in my own way too, but I was way more outgoing than my sister. At least that's how Adam remembers it. "Simone was this tiny little thing, but she had this big, bright, bubbly personality, and always a huge smile on her face," he tells others now. "She was just bouncing all over the place with this really high-pitched, really loud voice. She couldn't quite control her volume at that point. And everything was just so fascinating to her. So if she started telling you a story, it was like she was going to burst with the excitement of it. That was just the way she spoke."

Adam was describing the cheerful, fun side of me, but I had another side. Yep. Even back then, I was just plain stubborn. The hardheadedness really kicked in at dinnertime. Grandma said we weren't allowed to get up from the table until we finished our food, so I'd sit there for hours upon hours until I started nodding off, my head drooping into the plate. The problem was I hated the chewiness of meat. And I wasn't really into veggies either. I'm more of a pasta and pizza kind of girl. Well, my grandma was convinced that meat and veggies were part of a healthy diet, and she'd insist I clean my plate. But it always seemed like more than I could eat, and besides, it was food I didn't *want* to eat.

Then I got a brilliant idea. When no one was looking, I'd take the food and stick it in a small, hollow space underneath my booster seat. My grandma never noticed until she went to clean the booster seat one day and ran into all this old food underneath it—mashed potatoes and meatloaf and chicken nuggets and carrots, all this gross stuff. She was so mad, she scraped the gunk onto a plate.

"Simone, you're going to eat every bite of this!" she said, sliding the plate in front of me at dinner. *Oh snap.*

"No!" I wailed.

Grandma was only trying to make a point about me wasting food, so of course, she eventually gave me my real dinner. Soon after, she decided our nightly mealtime battles just weren't worth it, and she started to puree my meat and serve it to me with noodles. I liked that much better.

Even with all our dinner table confrontations, I adored my grandparents and I was quickly making friends in the neighborhood. All of us were starting to thrive. Then one afternoon, about eight months later, we got home from school to a familiar but unexpected face.

——•——

CHAPTER 3

True Home

"You don't choose your family. They are
God's gift to you, as you are to them."

—Desmond Tutu, human rights activist

M ama!" Ashley and Tevin both yelled, running to Shanon and wrapping skinny brown arms around her waist. My stomach felt as if a hundred frantic butterflies were flapping their wings inside me. I could see how much my brother and sister had missed Shanon and how much she'd missed them. They were all laughing and crying, their voices loud and blending together as they greeted one another. I don't think anyone noticed how quiet I was, standing off to the side. I was only three years old, but I knew right then that our calm, predictable life in Spring was about to change. Maybe that's why I hung back.

Since I hadn't lived with Shanon as long as Ashley and Tevin had, I barely remembered her. Adria didn't know Shanon at all. She was only six months old when we went into foster care, and she wasn't yet two when Shanon showed up that day. My little sister held on to our grandma, her tiny fists grabbing the cloth of her blouse, her face pressed against her shoulder.

I learned later that Shanon had called to ask my grandparents if she could come to see us. At first, my grandma was hesitant. She didn't think it was a good idea, because life in Texas was going along smoothly and she didn't want to disrupt our routine. The way she saw it, we'd had enough disruption to last a lifetime. But Grandpa didn't see the harm in letting Shanon visit. He wanted to see her too, to make sure his daughter really was doing better than before.

A couple of days later, when Shanon started talking about trying to reunite the family, I didn't know how to feel. Ashley and Tevin wanted to be with her, and as much as I'd grown to love and depend on my grandparents, I wanted to be with my brother and sister. I didn't know the world without them. I felt so torn.

Grandpa talked things over with the social worker, because he was worried about how Adria and I would manage if things spun out of control again. "What if we send the two older ones back and keep the younger ones here," he suggested. "If things start to unravel, at least Ashley and Tevin are old enough to call us."

The social worker told Grandpa that he needed to keep us together, which meant we'd either all go back to Columbus or we'd all stay in Spring. To my grandparents, the answer seemed simple: all four of us would remain with them. But over the next few months, it became more and more clear that Ashley and Tevin wanted to be back with Shanon, and so the decision was made for all four of us to return to Ohio. I could tell that Grandma and Grandpa were sad to see us leave, but they prayed for the best.

"I'd formed such a bond with the children," Grandma said years later. "It was so hard to say good-bye. I remember we were trying to give them all advice about things, especially the older ones, right up until the last minute. My heart was going out the door with them."

The following winter, Grandpa flew with us back to Columbus. The strange thing was we didn't go straight to Shanon's house. Instead, child protective services placed us back in the home of the foster family we'd been with before. The social worker wanted to oversee our transition and make sure Shanon was actually up to taking care of us.

We never did go back to live with Shanon, because she kept failing her drug tests. The social worker told her that if she could just pass a few tests in a row, they'd let us move back in with her. But she couldn't seem to stay sober. Finally, after another year of this, child services terminated Shanon's parental rights and put us up for adoption. Grandpa wanted all four of us to come back to Texas, but Ashley and Tevin didn't want to leave Ohio; they wanted to stay close to Shanon. After a lot of back and forth with child services and our extended family, it was decided that Ashley and Tevin would move to Cleveland to live with Grandpa's older sister, Aunt Harriet, and she would adopt them. As for Adria and me, we would return to Spring to live with our grandparents. This time, for good.

—=—

In bringing us back to Spring, and then adopting us, my grandma was doing what she'd seen her own parents do. Grandma was born in Belize City, Belize, where she also grew up. She had two sisters and a brother, and they all had a comfortable upbringing as the children of a senator who was also a deacon in the Catholic Church. Her family prayed the rosary together every day, led by her father, and they attended church every Sunday. Because of her father's government position, and the grocery store that her mother ran in the downstairs of their home, Grandma Nellie always had what she needed. But she had cousins and other family members who weren't as fortunate. Her mother would take these relatives into their home during hard times. My grandma remembers growing up with lots of cousins around, and they're as close as siblings to this day. I'm sure my grandma got her big heart and devotion to family from her parents.

Grandma left Belize and came to America when she was eighteen. She'd been accepted into a nursing school in San Antonio, Texas, and her parents were doing well enough to pay for their children's college education in the States. My grandpa came from a world very different from Grandma's, but with the same strong values and love for family. Grandpa is one of nine children, and he grew up in the housing projects in Cleveland. He joined the air force soon after he graduated from high school, and he and my grandma first met when he was stationed at a military base in San Antonio. My grandma was in her junior year of studying nursing at Incarnate Word College, and she'd gone with a girlfriend to a party. Grandpa was at the same party with his brother, and they all started talking. And you know what's funny? My grandma ended up marrying my grandpa, and Grandma Nellie's friend ended up marrying Grandpa Ron's brother!

When my grandparents met, Shanon was five years old and she'd been living with my grandpa in Texas. My grandparents wanted to adopt her, but of course, Shanon's mom wanted to keep her daughter close. Soon after the wedding, Shanon's mom sent for her to come back to Ohio. Now, all these years later, my sister and I were reversing that journey and heading from Ohio to Texas.

Adria and I came back to Spring on Christmas Eve 2002. I was five and my sister was three. Grandma was a little worried about me at first: She noticed I was a lot more guarded than before. I was still bouncy and hyper, and I still acted like a little mother to Adria, but I was less talkative. Years later, Grandma told me that she thought it was because I was afraid to trust the situation, because we'd lived with them before and then they'd let us go. She thought I might be wondering whether she and Grandpa were going to send us back to Ohio again. All I remember is being really glad to be back in Spring. It was like my own Christmas miracle.

Even though my grandparents started the process of adopting Adria and me as soon as we got back, we still called them Grandma and Grandpa. For the next year, social workers made regular home and school visits to make sure we were bonding properly. Meanwhile, Grandma enrolled our family in counseling to get us through the transition and bring us together. To my grandmother, making us her own children meant she would lay down her life for us without even thinking about it. She wanted us to know we could rely on her and my grandpa one hundred percent. And you know what? I did feel that I could depend on them. At a certain point, we all broke through to a deep-down understanding that we were a family. We belonged to each other. They were mine now, and I was theirs, even though the court didn't formally approve our adoption for another year.

On November 7, 2003, our family went down to the courthouse to finalize the adoption. In the judge's chambers, there was Grandpa, Grandma, Adria, and me (Ron II and Adam were both away at school). I was now six and Adria was four, and we were both wearing dresses. Back then, other than my baby dolls and Barbies, I didn't like girly-girly stuff. I would roll out of bed in the morning and grab my favorite pair of overalls, then head right for the trampoline in the backyard. But that day in court, I was wearing a very girly dress in my favorite color, blue, with my hair done up in two braids held by matching plastic barrettes. My little sister was dressed like a mini me, except her dress was pink, which is still her favorite color. My grandma had on her pearl earrings and a gold chain necklace, and my grandpa wore his usual work clothes. Something about the way we all stood with our lawyers and the social worker in front of the judge told me this was a very important day.

That evening, after dinner, Adria and I got up from the table to head upstairs and get ready for bed. That was our usual routine.

"Good night, Grandma!" I called as I was skipping out of the kitchen with Adria on my heels.

Grandma, who was at the sink rinsing dishes to stack in the dishwasher, stopped and looked at us. She had a funny expression on her face, which made Adria and me pause in the doorway and look back at her, waiting.

Grandma wiped her hands on a dishtowel and said, "Simone, Adria, come here."

There was something different in her tone. I didn't know what to expect.

"You know, girls," she said as we stood in front of her, "we adopted you both today. So I'm your mother now, and he"—she pointed at my grandpa, who was wiping the table mats—"he's your father."

Grandpa paused what he was doing, stood up straight, and smiled. I just glanced from one to the other, my eyes big and round. What had happened in court that day suddenly became clear.

"Does that mean I can call you Mom and Dad?" I asked.

"It's up to you," my grandma said, one hand cupping my cheek, the other one smoothing Adria's hair. "Call us whatever you want to. Now go to bed."

The two of us scampered upstairs without another word.

But when Adria went into the bathroom to brush her teeth, I stood in the middle of our bedroom, my hands pressed against my temples. I was hopping from one foot to the other and jumping up and down, so much excitement was flowing through me.

Mom. Dad. Mom. Dad.

I kept whispering the words, getting used to the sound of them. Finally, feeling as if I would burst, I ran back downstairs and to the kitchen.

"Mom?" I said, standing in the doorway.

She looked across at me, her lips twitching like she was trying not to smile.

"Yes, Simone?"

I turned to where Grandpa was putting away the table mats.

"Dad?"

"What is it, Simone?"

"Nothing!" I said, squealing and bouncing up and down gleefully.

I had done it—I'd called them Mom and Dad!

I turned without another word and raced back up the stairs. In my room, I flopped backward onto my bed and let out a happy sigh. Adria and I were finally and forever *home*.

———

Shanon still calls Adria and me on birthdays and holidays, but we don't have much contact beyond that. Some days, I feel a little bit sad for her. It's not that I ever wanted to go back to live in Ohio, but I do wish she'd been able to make better decisions when she was younger. I'm glad that she's now working so hard to stay clean. Every now and then, I think about how my life might've been different if Shanon had been able to keep us with her. If I'd stayed in Ohio, would I have ever gotten into gymnastics? Probably so, because I truly believe I was supposed to take this journey, which means God would have made a way. But when it comes to how things turned out, I'm not sorry. I'm part of a beautiful family that is closer and more loving than any I could've ever chosen. As the woman told my grandma—now my mom—in the lunch break room all those years ago, God never makes a mistake.

CHAPTER 4

Doing Backflips

"The unexpected is usually what brings the unbelievable."

—MANDY KELLOGG RYE, WRITER

Out of the corner of my eye, I noticed one of our day care teachers opening the closet where our bright blue "Kids R Kids" T-shirts were neatly folded on a shelf. The minute she started taking piles of the shirts into her arms, I ran to her side, and so did the other kids, almost seventy of us crowding around. The teacher handed out the shirts, and we quickly shrugged into them, screeching excitedly. We all knew what blue T-shirts meant: field trip day! *Where*, I wondered, *would we be going today?* I stared across the room at my big brother Adam, looking for a clue.

Ron II and Adam had both been teachers at the day care Adria and I attended. That summer, Adam was working at the center part-time while going to community college, where he was studying business. I soon noticed that Adam's eyebrows were all scrunched up as if he was trying to work out something in his mind. I followed his gaze and saw that he was scowling at the pouring rain outside the window. I watched as he and our other lead teacher huddled together with the four assistant teachers. Finally, they called all the kids over.

"Okay, everyone, listen up," Adam said. "We were supposed to go to a farm in the country today. But since it's raining so hard, we're taking you to a tumbling gym instead."

Adam was the one who'd suggested Bannon's Gymnastix for the field trip. It was just down the street from the day care, and he knew his little sisters would enjoy it way more than going to, say, a museum, where we'd have to be quiet and orderly—two things that never came easy for me! Also, it didn't hurt that I absolutely loved doing backflips and somersaults. My brothers actually used to bounce me off the trampoline to see how high I'd fly and how many flips I could do before I landed. It drove our mom insane. I was so small and light that she was worried they'd bounce me so hard I'd get hurt. But I'd laugh and tell her, "Mom, it's fun!" I loved roughhousing with my brothers, trying out different moves, and figuring out how to land on my feet.

By this time, I'd become a world-class climber. At home, I liked to see how fast I could crawl up and sit on my brothers' shoulders while they were standing. And one of my favorite games was to make a running start and grab on to their outstretched arms to see how many pull-ups I could do before I'd drop back down and keep running. I must have been an exhausting six-year-old! Adam probably figured I'd be easier to supervise while tumbling around and doing my usual backyard tricks on Bannon's enormous spring floors. I could land with no danger of injuring myself on the padded mats or in the squishy foam pits.

The minute I got inside Bannon's, I saw all kinds of equipment made for just my size—low beams and low bars and floor vaults that I was eager to try. I watched a gymnast do a back handspring skill on the vault, and I immediately wanted to try out the same move on the kiddie springboard. I let loose, going from one apparatus to the other, trying to copy skills I saw the older gymnasts practicing in the gym. After a while, Adam came over to me.

"Simone, do a flip," he said. "Let me see you do a flip."

"I'll do one if you do it first," I challenged him.

"Okay," he said. He did a backflip, but instead of landing on his feet, he crashed right onto his butt. When he saw me laughing at him, he was like, "Okay, smarty-pants, if you can do it better then show me."

My brothers know how much I love a challenge, so Adam probably knew I'd go for broke. I did a backflip with a little twist on the layout and then I did it again, landing upright on my feet.

Right then, a lady from the gym came over to talk to us. We'd seen her at the receptionist's desk earlier when we first came in. The whole time I'd been jumping and flipping and swinging from the low bars, she'd been watching me from across the room.

"My name is Veronica," she said to Adam, "but people call me Ronnie. Is this your daughter?" she asked, nodding toward me.

"Whoa! I'm no one's dad," said Adam, who would soon turn nineteen. "This is my little sister."

"Has she had any formal gymnastics training?" Ronnie asked.

"No," he said. "Not a single class."

While they were talking, I got bored and began to do some more flips into the foam pit. Ronnie immediately started coaching me on the proper form. "Point your toes, Simone," she called out to me. "Keep your knees together."

Turning back to Adam, she said, "Do you want to sign her up for classes?"

"I'm not the one to make that decision," Adam told her. "You're going to have to talk to our parents."

That's how I arrived home from our field trip with a letter inviting me to enroll in gymnastics or tumbling classes at Bannon's.

"Mom, they gave me this letter for you," I said, placing the sheet of paper on the kitchen counter. I tilted my head to one side and added, "I really want to go back to that gym." Then I ran up the stairs to my room to wash up before dinner.

Mom didn't see the letter as anything special at first. She

figured that all the kids who visited Bannon's probably got such flyers as part of the gym's marketing strategy. But that letter *was* special in another way: because of it, a lightbulb went off in my mom's head.

"Never in my wildest dreams did I think to put the girls in gymnastics," Mom admitted years later. "Even though they would jump on that trampoline for hours on end, the sport just wasn't part of my experience. Growing up in Belize, we'd watch gymnastics when the Olympics came around, and that was all."

Now, suddenly, Mom realized that recreational gymnastics might be the perfect outlet for her daughters—especially for me, her little bouncing bean who jumped and climbed on everything nonstop. She called me back downstairs and sat me down at the kitchen table, across from her.

"Simone," she said, "this letter you brought home, they're asking if you want to do gymnastics or tumbling classes."

"What's the difference?" I asked.

"Well, as far as I understand it, gymnastics is all four events that you saw today—the bar, the vault, the beam, and the floor—but tumbling, well, I think you just get to tumble. You just do the floor separately."

"I want to do all four," I announced.

—————

Mom signed Adria and me up for recreational gymnastics classes that very week. She enrolled us in forty-five-minute sessions twice a week, and she bought us colorful leos from

Bannon's gift shop on our first day. I couldn't have been more thrilled. I was finally learning the proper way to do all those skills I used to improvise on the trampoline. Adria was more lukewarm about the whole experience. She just went along with me.

Ronnie was the recreational gymnastics coach. Halfway through our first class, she called over another teacher to run the session for a few minutes so she could find her daughter, Aimee Boorman, who was one of Bannon's team coaches.

"You have to come see this little kid," Ronnie told Aimee. "She's a natural."

Aimee had been involved in gymnastics since she was six, which meant Ronnie had also spent almost three decades immersed in the sport, first as a gymnastics mom and later as a coach. Ronnie *knew* gymnastics. She told us later that she just "had a sense" about me.

But Aimee was busy coaching and blew her off.

"Mom, I can't right now," she said.

Ronnie insisted. "Aimee, you *want* to see this kid. She has . . . *something.*"

"Mooom," Aimee said, sounding exasperated. "Okay, okay, in a bit."

Aimee never came to see me that day, or for the next two classes. Then toward the end of my second week, she was walking through the gym to the area where the team gymnasts practiced, and she noticed me. "I saw this teeny, petite thing with rippling muscles who was just full of energy and couldn't stay still," Aimee said later. "She was sitting on the floor with her legs out in front of her. Then she put her hands at her sides and pulled up through her stomach, just on her hands, and I thought, *Hmm, six-year-olds shouldn't be able to do that.* Later, during that same class, she was on a mat waiting in line for her turn, and the mat was four inches thick, and she did a seat drop and bounced right back up to her feet as if she was on a trampoline. I was like, *Okay, that's not normal.*"

After the class, Aimee cornered her mom to ask her who I was.

"Aimee," Ronnie said, "that's the kid I wanted you to see!" Nobody could have guessed back then that Aimee would one day become my coach.

Soon after, Adria and I moved into Bannon's USAG Junior Olympic (JO) program, which allows gymnasts to advance through ten skill levels and compete in district, state, regional, and—ultimately—national competitions. We were now officially on Bannon's Jet Star team, which was the name of our age group. But only a month later, Adria dropped out of gymnastics and joined Girl Scout Brownies instead. She said she didn't like people watching her perform. That wasn't the case for me. I wanted my coaches to see that even though I was small, I wasn't scared to tackle the big skills.

A few times a year, Bannon's would hold recitals for the students at each level so that parents and families could see what we were learning. At my first recital, held just a few weeks after I joined the JO program, we were supposed to perform basic conditioning exercises. One of the skills was a seated rope climb, where we sat next to a dangling rope and climbed it for about ten feet using only our arms. We did this while keeping our legs straight out in a seated position.

Adam remembers that I clambered up that rope and got to the required height of ten feet really fast—and then I looked around and kept climbing! I was like fifteen or twenty feet in the air, swinging from the rope up toward the ceiling and laughing. Even as a six-year-old, I had such crazy upper body strength that it was always easy for me. People at the bottom of the rope were shouting up to me, "Okay, Simone, you're good, come down now. No, seriously, come down here!" It was so much fun! To this day, I love a rope climb.

I was still very young, so I don't recall much about that recital, but Adam says that I also did a vault exercise. The way Adam remembers it, we all ran down a runway and hit a little springboard, then did a handstand into a layout. Most of the kids hit the springboard and landed near the front of the mat. However, I hit the springboard with so much power that I propelled myself all the way to the back of the mat. All the coaches looked up when I landed. They were like, "Well, she *really* vaulted!"

At the end of that recital, everybody got a trophy for participating. But from then on, my training shifted into high gear. The very next week, my coaches moved me straight to level four. Then, a couple of weeks later, they began training me on level five skills and signed me up for my first competitive season, which ran from August to November. In the JO program, in order to move up to a new level, you have to either earn a particular score in competition or place high enough in a qualifying meet, depending on the rules for that level. Levels four, five, and six were the compulsory levels. Every gymnast had to perform the same routine, which was set by the USAG and showcased all the skills you had to master for each level. At level five, the rundown of compulsory skills looked like this:

VAULT: Front handspring

BARS: Kip; cast to above horizontal bar; clear hip to above horizontal bar; back sole circle to clear front support or back stalder circle to clear front support; backward sole circle; squat on; long hang kip; long hang pullover; tap swings; flyaway dismount

BEAM: Back walkover or back extension roll or back handspring step out; straight leg leap to 150 degrees; split jump; sissonne; cartwheel to side handstand, quarter-turn dismount

FLOOR: Straddle jump; stretch jump with full turn; front handspring step out, front handspring to two feet; front tuck; leap (150 degrees); full turn; round-off back handspring back tuck

If you've never done gymnastics, that might look like a hard list or maybe even like a different language. But those are just the basic skills that every gymnast builds on. When I first got to Bannon's, I could already do some of those skills, thanks to Ron and Adam bouncing me off the trampoline and Tevin teaching me backflips off the backyard swing. Of course, I didn't have a clue what any of the moves were called, and my form and shape definitely weren't on point. I lacked polish—the finishing details like pointed toes, knees pressed together, graceful hands, and full extensions through my arms and legs. But I did have two things going for me: I was fearless and eager to learn.

Luckily, my coaches thought I had enough raw ability to move up quickly through the levels. It helped that I was a visual learner. I could look at someone doing a skill and quickly copy it. I also had an inborn sense of where I was as I tumbled through air. "Simone has incredible air balance," Aimee told my mom. "She can feel exactly where she is in space while flipping and twisting, and she knows instinctively just how to bring her feet down so that she lands upright. That's something no coach can teach."

Aimee likes to tell this one story about me: In one of my early JO classes when I had just turned seven, I saw a member of the cheerleading team do a standing back tuck. So I ran over to the gymnastics coaches—Aimee, Susan, and Selinda—and said, "I can do that."

Aimee looked down at this tiny little person eagerly smiling up at her.

"No, you can't," she said.

I insisted, "Yeah, I can." And then I did it.

All three coaches just stared at me.

Then Susan challenged, "I bet you can't do it on the beam."

I said, "Sure!" then ran over and jumped up onto the high beam, which was taller than I was at the time. As I was getting ready to do a standing back tuck, the coaches were running over and yelling, "Nooooo! Simone, get off the high beam! That's too high for you! Get down!" Susan said, "Okay, Simone, come over here and try it on floor beam."

So I hopped down and ran over to the low beam. And I pulled it off.

Years later, Aimee told me that was the day she knew I had what it took to go all the way—to Nationals, to Worlds, and, one day, maybe even to the Olympics.

CHAPTER 5

Shady Arbor Way

"We make each other stronger.
That ain't ever gonna change."

—FROM THE FILM *THE CHEETAH GIRLS*

Say it loud, I'm black and I'm proud!"

Every morning, while driving us to school, Adam would put that James Brown song on the car radio. He'd turn up the volume, start bopping his head, tapping the steering wheel, and singing along.

"Come on, Simone and Adria, sing!" he'd yell, and the

two of us would jump in, drumming our hands on the back of the car seat and belting out the words as Adam yelled, "Louder! Louder!" Our morning music jam with our brother was like our own little dance party before school. By the time we rolled into the parking lot, we were two happy little girls, the beat still playing in our heads.

Little did we know Adam was using that song to instill pride in us, since most of the children we went to school and gym with looked different from us. Adam wanted us to be happy and confident in ourselves, no matter where we were. But at five and seven years old, Adria and I didn't think twice about that. All we cared about was the way that song got our hearts pumping and our day started off just right. Still, maybe his message got through, because Adria and I always felt completely comfortable growing up in Spring and traveling around our home state, Texas.

By this time, I'd been in gymnastics for about a year. Back then, our family lived on a street called Shady Arbor Way, and our house was at the end of a cul-de-sac. "Stay where I can see you!" Mom would call out from the window at the front of our house. Adria and I rolled our eyes, but we always made sure to stay within the concrete circle of the cul-de-sac. Our mom and dad were pretty strict compared to our friends' parents. They didn't allow Adria and me to attend sleepover parties or go on play dates with anyone but our cousins. And going to the mall to meet friends—even when we got older—made absolutely no sense to them. As far as they were concerned, young kids wandering aimlessly around a mall were just asking for trouble.

The silver lining was that Adria and I grew up as close as two sisters could be. We became champions at entertaining ourselves. We'd play jump rope, soccer, and hopscotch in that cul-de-sac, or we'd ride our bikes round and round, making zooming noises as if they were motorcycles. Adria also had a little motorized Barbie Jeep and I had a play Hummer, and we'd drive those toy cars endlessly around the circle. We'd put our Barbies and baby dolls next to us and act like we were moms coming home from work. We'd drive to the different mailboxes in the circle as if we were checking the mail. Sometimes, one of us would act like a cop chasing the other one. We'd pull the Jeep or the Hummer over and whip out a pretend notebook from our Hello Kitty purse and write a fake ticket.

On rainy days, we'd play tic-tac-toe for hours or watch *Power Puff Girls* marathons on TV. On sunny days, we'd invent fun activities like the "Trying Not to Laugh" game, which we'd play on the covered patio behind our house. One of us would take a big mouthful of water, and then the other one would set a kitchen timer and try to get the first one to laugh in thirty seconds or less. The whole point of the game was to make the other person laugh so hard that water comes spurting out of her mouth, like in movies when someone's caught off guard. That game never got old. A couple of years ago, we even made a YouTube video of us playing it. As usual, I giggled a lot but held on to my mouthful of water. But when it was my turn, I made Adria laugh and spew water in less than ten seconds!

The only exception to the cul-de-sac rule was if we

asked to leave the circle to go to our friend Becca's house, which was a few doors down. Becca was Adria's age, and she was one of our two BFFs on the street. The other one was Marissa, who lived next door and was two days older than I was. During weekends and school holidays, the four of us were inseparable, racing in and out of each other's yards and making up games on the fly.

One of our favorites was acting like we were Cheetah Girls. The TV musical *The Cheetah Girls*, about four girls in a band at a performing arts high school in New York City, had just come out. Adria, Marissa, Becca, and I could not get enough of that movie. We watched the DVD almost every day one summer, and when the "Cheetah Sisters" song came on, we'd line up, hold our fists like mics, and sing and dance our hearts out, each of us taking on the role of our favorite Cheetah Girl.

I was Galleria. That was a no brainer, not only because we were both brown-skinned, but also because the name of the actress who played her was Raven-*Symone*. Marissa chose Chanel as her Cheetah Girl because they both had brown, curly hair, while Becca was Dorinda because she was dark blond, like her. The fourth Cheetah, Aquanette—Aqua for short—was brown-skinned like Galleria; Adria played her. In the movie, the girls all rock stylish animal print clothing as they try to become music superstars. I think pretending to be Galleria is why I love zebra prints to this day. The four of us were *serious* about being Cheetah Girls. We stepped into our imaginary roles every single day for an entire summer and into the new school year—at least until the incident with the clubhouse.

———

Adria and I ran down the street toward Becca's house, our flip-flops squishing into the water-soaked grass of our neighbors' lawn. It was late September, and Hurricane Rita had recently flooded Southern Texas. Like most families, Becca's parents had nailed sheets of plywood over their windows and glass doors to protect against the storm. Now that the hurricane had blown over, Becca's dad had ripped the wood off the house and piled it up against the garage. Adria and I found Becca and Marissa sorting through the pile and stacking the largest sheets of plywood on the damp grass.

"We're going to build a fort!" Marissa squealed as soon as she saw us.

"It can be our clubhouse!" I said.

We each ran back to our houses to rifle through our parents' toolboxes for hammers and nails. At the last second, I also grabbed a can of green paint and a paintbrush, thinking we could make a little sign to go over the doorway—*Cheetah Girls Clubhouse*.

Every afternoon for the next three days, the four of us gathered in Becca's backyard to continue hammering and nailing those pieces of plywood together. We'd get to work as soon as we got home from school, not even stopping to have a snack. Finally, we had a structure big enough for the four of us to fit. We even built a little bench to sit on inside the fort, and we had a plan to paint animal spots on the walls. I have to admit the structure did look a little rough, with huge gaps in the walls and a tilt to one side, but at least it stayed standing. We were so impressed with what we'd built as we crawled through the doorway and settled ourselves inside.

What we didn't know was that a spider had also settled itself near the ceiling. Sitting cross-legged, the four of us began belting out the "Cheetah Sister" song, shimmying our shoulders and slapping hands against our knees. We must have disturbed the spider, causing it to fall and land squarely on Marissa's head.

"Aaaah!" she screamed. She jumped up from the bench and brushed her hair and stamped her feet, then waved her arms around frantically. She scrambled outside the fort, still shrieking. Not knowing what was happening, the rest of us followed her out. When she told us about the spider, we all started cracking up. Her reaction had been so extreme that we couldn't help ourselves. We were rolling on the damp grass, holding our sides and giggling at Marissa's freak-out. I guess we were laughing so hard, we didn't notice that Marissa didn't find the whole thing funny.

"Stupid spider," Marissa grumbled, glaring at us. When we finally realized she was really upset, we tried to get serious but we didn't do it very well. You know how when you start laughing sometimes and your eyes start to water and you just can't stop? It was like that. Trying to cover up our giggling, Becca suggested we go play at Marissa's house, and she and I walked ahead down the driveway. At the gate, we turned to wait for Marissa and Adria, who were still up by the garage.

Suddenly, I saw Marissa punch my sister! Adria immediately started bawling. Before I knew what I was doing, I raced up the driveway and jumped on top of Marissa, shoving her down onto the grass.

"Don't you ever hit my sister again!" I yelled, my hands pinning Marissa's to the ground, my face inches from hers. I don't know what came over me. All I knew was that Adria was crying. It was like she was two years old again, and I was her protector, just as Tevin had once been mine. That feeling of wanting to take care of Adria was so strong in me that day. It's a feeling that I don't think will ever go away.

The next day at school, Marissa apologized to us; I apologized too. Just like that, the four of us were buddies again, although now that I think about it, we never really spent much time inside our fort. That sneaky spider ruined our Cheetah Girls fantasy. But it didn't destroy our friendship. Marissa and Becca are still two of my BFFs to this day.

———

One afternoon, Mom surprised Adria and me by saying we could ride our bikes as far as the stop sign at the other end of the street. We were super excited. All afternoon, we biked up and down the street, and when we got tired of riding our bikes, we just skipped back and forth to the stop sign, relishing our new freedom. Eventually the streetlights came on. One of Momma Biles's ironclad rules was that no matter where we were or what we were doing, once the streetlights came on, it was time to head home.

Just a few houses away from ours, next to the yard of two neighborhood boys named Trent and Grant, something blue glinted under the streetlight. We moved closer to investigate and found three blue eggs, two of them whole and the third one crushed and leaking yellow liquid, like a broken yolk.

"Oh no," Adria wailed. "The poor baby bird."

That's when I got an idea.

"Let's save them so the babies can hatch," I said, reaching down to pick up one of the good blue eggs.

"You mean, take them home with us?" Adria gave me a confused look.

"We'll protect them," I said with all the confidence of a seven-year-old with a plan. "Out here, they'll just break like the other egg."

Adria still wasn't convinced, but she followed my lead and scooped up a blue egg, holding it carefully against her chest. Back at home, we called out hello to Mom and Dad and scurried up the stairs to our bedroom before they could ask us what we were carrying. We fished out a pink plastic, octagonal container that was part of a pet shop play set, and we placed the two blue eggs inside. Adria filled the container with warm water and closed the lid. We put the container under the sink and hoped that the water would soothe the soon-to-be-hatched baby birds.

The next morning, we checked on the eggs. They looked fine. So we changed the water and went to school. In the afternoon, we went out to play with Marissa and Becca for a while. Then around four, when Becca's mom called her to come home, the other three of us went to my house to check on the eggs. When Adria took the container from under the sink this time, we noticed a yellow blur seeping out from the eggs and clouding the water.

Adria and I gasped, hands over our mouths, eyes wide and sad.

"What's the matter?" Marissa asked us, clearly confused.

"We killed the baby birds," Adria cried.

"What?" Marissa said, elbowing us aside and peering into the pink container. "Let me see." And then it was Marissa's turn to laugh at Adria and me. She laughed just as hard as we had laughed when the spider fell on her. "Those aren't bird eggs!" she told us, trying to catch her breath. "Those are paintball pods! Trent and Grant play paintball with them all the time!"

My sister and I might have felt a little silly right then, except that we were too busy gulping big sighs of relief.

Our parents never did find out about those blue eggs, just as they never knew about the turtle we found on the road one day, after a car had crushed it. I loved turtles. Maybe it was because my mom sometimes called me her "little turtle." I'd even started a figurine collection and was always on the look-out for new turtles to add to it whenever we traveled. Adria had a soft spot for turtles too, but I was surprised when she ran into the empty street and picked up the flattened thing.

"Adria, it's dead!" I hissed from the sidewalk.

"No," she said, "it can come back to life."

I don't know why we thought water would cure everything—maybe it was because in church, when you were baptized or made your first holy communion, they poured holy water on your head and you were healed. That's the only reason I can think of for why Adria and I submerged this squished turtle in water in the very same pet shop container we'd used to save the bird eggs. Once again, we left the container in our bathroom and checked on it every day. Adria (who, in her defense, was still only five years old) seemed convinced that the turtle would come back to life. But all that happened was that our bathroom began to reek. The smell was disgusting, and when it started invading our room, my sister had no choice but to throw that poor turtle away.

Even though Momma and Poppa Biles were on the strict side, they were really good about giving us space to play and explore—which is how we ended up with a smelly squished turtle in our bathroom. Most of the time, they waved off our exploits as childhood fun, but one time we got into a heap of trouble.

Adria and I were playing in the backyard, jumping on the trampoline, which was still my favorite activity. From the air, I spied a particular rock lying in the rose garden by the fence. It was larger than the pebbles around it, and it looked out of place, as if someone had left it there by accident.

I stopped jumping and went over to investigate. *This doesn't belong here,* I decided. And without thinking, I hurled the rock over the high wooden fence at the back of the yard.

Splash!

I froze.

"What was *that?*" Adria asked. "Is there a pool over there?"

Before I could answer, Adria had jumped down off the trampoline, picked up a stone, and threw it over the fence.

Another splash. We both started giggling.

I still can't explain why throwing stones over the fence and waiting for the splash seemed like fun to us. But it did. After a while, we started climbing on top of the fence so we'd get better aim and make sure our rocks landed in the water every time. The pool area and the backyard of that house were always deserted, so Adria and I thought our new game was harmless.

Later, we found out our rocks were getting into the pool filter and killing it, but because no one ever saw us throwing rocks in the pool, the man who lived there thought his dog was dropping stones into the water. Then one day, he *did* see us. When we climbed up on top of the fence, arms raised to hurl our rocks, the man was lying next to the pool, tanning on a lounge chair. He must've heard the commotion of us climbing, because when our heads popped over the top of the fence, he was staring straight at us!

"You're the ones throwing rocks in my pool!" he shouted, his face red.

Adria and I jumped down from the fence, dropped our rocks in the rose garden, and ran back inside our house as fast as we could. But not before we heard the man call out, "I'm coming over there to talk to your parents!"

Hearts pounding, my sister and I dug out our Barbie Dream House from the closet and acted as if we'd been inside playing Barbies all along. "Okay, he's not going to come." Under our breath, we tried to reassure one another. "He's not going to come, he's not going to—"

Right then, our front doorbell rang. We jumped to our feet and yelled over the stairway bannister, "Don't answer it! It's nobody!" Why we thought that would work, I'll never know.

Mom opened the door, and there was the man, standing there.

"I think your kids have been throwing rocks in my pool," he said.

Mom looked up at us peeking over the bannister and said, "Is that true?"

I hate to admit it, but we flat-out lied, shaking our heads vigorously from left to right. The man looked at us in disbelief. "I just *saw* you!"

"You girls did ask if you could play outside," Mom said, looking at us hard.

After the man left, we got the scolding of our lives, not just for throwing rocks in the man's pool, but also for lying about it. Strangely, Mom didn't seem that angry with us, just very disappointed, which made me feel so much worse. As she talked to us that day, we learned two very important lessons. First, always have the courage to own up to your mistakes. And second, respect other people's property. Actually, Adria and I also came up with a third lesson: a true Cheetah Girl never lies.

CHAPTER 6

A Novena

"Love begins by taking care of the closest ones—the ones at home."

—MOTHER TERESA, CATHOLIC MISSIONARY

"So how would you kids feel about Grandma living here?" It was Good Friday 2004, and that out-of-the-blue question was how Mom announced that Grandma Everista Cayetano (pronounced *Kai-ee-tano*) would be leaving Belize and moving in with us.

"When is she coming?" I wanted to know because I adored our grandmother. Mom didn't have a date yet. She explained that Grandma Caye (as her grandkids called her) had been taking care of our grandpa Silas after he'd had a stroke, but now she was suffering from health problems of her own. Mom had decided to bring Grandma Caye to Texas, where she could get some much-needed medical attention and a few months of rest before returning home. But first, Mom had to find a caretaker in Belize who could move into the house with Grandpa Silas to take care of him while Grandma was away.

We were sitting at the kitchen table when Mom told us this plan. Ron and Adam were both home from college to spend Easter with the family. We'd just returned from Good Friday services at St. Ignatius Loyola Catholic Church, and were about to perform my favorite Biles family ritual—tie-dying eggs for our annual Easter egg hunt. In front of us sat two dozen hard-boiled eggs in a bowl. Next to them were six smaller bowls, each one holding a different color of liquid food dye. When we were done, our brothers would hide twelve eggs for Adria and twelve for me to find on Easter Sunday. I could hardly wait.

Distracted by coloring the eggs, I didn't think much about exactly why Grandma Caye was leaving Belize. Mom explained that she had pulmonary fibrosis, and it was getting worse, but I was seven years old, and *pulmonary fibrosis* were two big, grown-up words I didn't understand. Instead, I focused on how much fun it would be to have Grandma with us all the time. I had such good memories of staying with her on family vacations in Belize, going to the beach with her and my cousins, going deep-sea fishing on a boat, doing backflips off the pier, or just hanging out in Grandma Caye's living room, bent over my Nintendo DS. Sometimes in the afternoons, my brothers, sister, and I would wait with Grandma Caye in the front yard until the ice cream man came by on his bicycle. Grandma Caye would buy orange, mango, or pineapple ice cream pops—still the best ice cream I've ever tasted. My mother would sit on the porch next to my dad and smile happily as we licked our ice cream. I loved how relaxed my mom always seemed in Belize and how her accent would come out stronger when she talked to Grandma Caye. Mom was her oldest child, and they'd always been close.

"How long is Grandma going to stay with us?" I asked as I dipped an egg in turquoise blue.

"Not sure," Mom said, her voice distant.

To me, this seemed like a chance for us to pamper Grandma Caye as she had always pampered us. I imagined bringing her breakfast in bed, snuggling up to her on the couch in the TV room, and seeing her in the viewing area with the rest of my family at gymnastics recitals. I was eager to show her all the new skills I was learning, and to introduce my friends on the Jet Stars team. I especially enjoyed knowing Grandma Caye would be waiting every day when I got home from school.

But when Grandma Caye arrived that summer, she was weaker and moved more slowly than she ever had. She stayed in bed a lot and was often out of breath. Still, she was always up for hugs and kisses and laughs, and she even came with us to one of my recitals at Bannon's.

That December, Grandma Caye insisted on flying back to Belize to spend Christmas with Grandpa Silas. They had talked on the phone every single day, and they missed each other terribly. My mom didn't think Grandma Caye was strong enough to travel and tried to talk her out of it. But if Grandma Caye got something in her head, it was hard to turn her around. In that way, we're just alike. I think Grandma Caye somehow knew that it would be her last Christmas at home in Belize with my grandpa.

When she returned to us in January, Grandma was even frailer, and she needed to be on oxygen all the time. But it wasn't until my aunt Corrine flew in from Maryland a few months later that I realized Grandma Caye was sicker than I knew. Mom had called everyone to say they should come soon if they wanted to see Grandma Caye, because she was getting close to the end. During the first two weeks of June, family members visited nonstop—my mom's cousin, Aunt Florita, from California; mom's other sister, Aunt Jennifer, from Arizona; and her brother, Uncle Silas, from Washington. Another of my mom's cousins, Aunt Anjelica, drove in from Huntsville, Texas, and Grandma's sister, Aunt Anjelina, also came. All the aunts and uncles brought their spouses and children, which meant the house was full of cousins of all ages running in and out. The atmosphere was so playful and lively that it was hard for us kids to understand why everyone was actually there.

Hoping for a miracle, my mom began praying a novena, which is a series of prayers asking for special graces from God. You repeat the prayers for nine days in a row, and by the end you're supposed to see a merciful shift in whatever situation you've been praying about. Mom wasn't expecting it when, on the eighth day, Grandma Caye called her into her room and said she was ready to die. Grandma had started speaking only in Spanish, her first language, as she became weaker, so I didn't understand a lot of what she was saying. My mom told me later that Grandma had decided to stop taking her medication and didn't want to go to the hospital.

"I want to stay here with you until my last breath," Grandma Caye told my mom on that eighth afternoon. "And I want you to know I am not afraid. God has shown me in my dreams just where I'm going, and I'm ready. I am at peace, Nellie, and I want all of you to be at peace too."

Mom didn't know what to say, so she kissed Grandma Caye's forehead and went to the kitchen and cried. This wasn't the miracle from God that she'd been praying for with her novena. She wasn't ready to let go of the woman who had so lovingly raised her and made her who she was. But the next morning, when Mom said the ninth and final prayer in her novena, a feeling of great peace came over her, and that's when she realized that the novena hadn't been for my grandma, but for her. Grandma already had God's grace, and now my mom was being filled with it too.

After her prayer, Mom went into my grandma's room. "Okay," she whispered, taking Grandma Caye's wrinkled hand in hers. "I will do what you ask. I will not force you to take your medicine. I will go on this journey with you."

Every night after that, my mom slept in the bed next to my grandma, knowing that each breath could be her last. Sometimes, Grandma Caye would wake up in the middle of the night and ask my mom, "Am I dead?" and my mom would say, "Not if you're talking to me!" Then they'd both laugh a little at that. Even in such a hard moment, my mother and grandmother kept their sense of humor. Watching them together, I felt so blessed to be a part of such a loving and closely bonded family.

One evening, Grandma Caye was having so much trouble breathing that we thought she was going to die that night, but she didn't. The next morning—June 11, 2005—Mom called everyone who was in the house into Grandma Caye's room, and we stood around her bed and said the rosary. Her breathing got easier as we prayed, and when we were done, I knelt on the side of the bed and put my arms around my grandma. "I love you, Grandma Caye," I said, resting my forehead against her cheek. She smiled and patted my shoulder weakly.

A short while later she started fighting for breath again, and Aunt Anjelina sent the cousins out of the room. "Just keep praying for your grandma," she told the six of us from the top of the stairs. "Please pray."

In the living room, we cousins made a circle around the coffee table and clasped our hands. "God, please let Grandma Caye be all right," we said over and over. Soon after, our mothers came downstairs. My mom's face was stained with tears as she held Adria and me. "Your grandma is with God now," she whispered. The four youngest of us started sobbing, not only because we'd lost Grandma Caye, but also because our own mothers were crying. To this day, if my mom breaks down, I will too.

The next week we all flew to Belize City for Grandma Caye's funeral. Adria and I knew that she had died, but we didn't quite understand that she was truly gone until we stood with the rest of the family at her graveside and watched her casket being lowered into the ground. As some men sprinkled dirt over Grandma Caye's casket, I looked up at my mom, who had tears on her cheeks. But she seemed calm, as if everything was happening the way it was supposed to happen. I leaned against her side as the priest announced the next hymn. Everyone started singing "Here I Am, Lord."

> *Here I am Lord, Is it I, Lord?*
> *I have heard You calling in the night.*
> *I will go Lord, if You lead me.*
> *I will hold Your people in my heart.*

I felt my mom's arm circle my shoulders and pull me close as I gazed up at the cloudless blue sky. I was picturing our beloved Grandma Caye in heaven, looking around and feeling peaceful in the presence of God, but still missing her family. I was sure she was happy that she'd insisted on one last Christmas with our grandpa.

After the funeral, Mom arranged to bring Grandpa Silas back to Texas with us, because she couldn't bear to leave him alone in Belize. She'd recently gone into a business arrangement to run several nursing homes, and she and her partners had already purchased and renovated six of them. Mom and Dad set Grandpa Silas up in a bright, sunny room in one of the nursing homes since he needed more intensive medical care than he'd be able to get at home.

My mom went to see him there every day, and the entire family visited him on Sundays after church. Adria and I would do wheelies in his wheelchair, which he wasn't too happy about. Since I was the ringleader, he'd try to distract me by asking what skills I was learning in gymnastics. Sometimes I'd demonstrate a back tuck or a tumbling move, and he'd say, "I was a great tumbler in my day. You get your gymnastics talent from me, Simone." I loved that he believed that. It was our own special connection.

Every Sunday, while sitting with Grandpa, we'd end up telling stories about Grandma Caye. We never stopped missing her. Maybe that's why Adria and I loved "Here I Am, Lord" so much; it became our favorite church song. Some nights before bedtime, we'd ask Mom to play the hymn for us on iTunes, then Adria and I would get in the bathtub, prop the little booklet from the funeral service on the side of the tub, and take turns singing. Though Grandma Caye was now in heaven with God, singing that hymn always made us feel closer to her, as if she was right there, still holding us in her heart.

CHAPTER 7

Leveling Up

*"Each of us has a fire in our hearts
for something. It's our goal in life
to find it and keep it lit."*

—MARY LOU RETTON,
THE 1984 OLYMPIC GYMNASTICS CHAMPION

I was stoked. Finally, I was learning how to do full rotations around the high bar with my body completely extended, starting at the top of the bar in a perfectly vertical handstand, legs together and toes pointed to the sky. The skill is called a giant, and it is crucial to a gymnastics career. The sooner I could master it, the sooner I'd be able to move on to harder dismounts and other big skills.

Coach Susan had spotted me in practice the day before, standing level with me on padded leather blocks stacked on one side of the foam pit. She kept one hand on my arm and the other flat on my back as I swung 360 degrees around the bar. Now I felt ready to try doing giants on my own. I'd already completed my conditioning stations for the afternoon—leg lifts and chin-ups on the ladder by the wall, rope climbs, sprints around the gym, sit ups, and push-ups, everything on Susan's list—so I headed over to the high bar.

I mounted the bar with a kip and swung myself up to the handstand. I'd completed two or three rotations when, suddenly, my grip slipped a little and I started toppling to one side. Usually, when we make a mistake like that on bars, we fall safely into the spongy foam underneath. But my fall that day was so bizarre that when I hit the high bar, I bounced off it and rolled down the steel cables at the side, landing hard on the concrete. *Ouch.*

Chest heaving, I lay on my back looking up at the vaulted ceiling of the gym. Tears spilled from the corners of my eyes. I knew how lucky I was to have escaped with no broken bones, but I'd been truly frightened. I was still on the ground thinking, *I'm never doing that again!* when I saw Coach Nicole standing over me.

"Get up, Simone."

I got to my feet and wiped my eyes. I was expecting a little sympathy, but, clearly, I'd misjudged Nicole. She was straight-faced and matter-of-fact as she stacked up several of the spotting blocks so that she could stand level with the bar. She climbed onto the padded blocks and stood waiting. I realized she expected me to get back up there.

"I'm not doing another giant!" I burst out.

"Come on, Simone," she said calmly. "Get up here."

"Did you see me just *fall?*"

"Get up here," she repeated.

"No!" I said, crying all over again. "I'm *not* doing it."

"Yes, you are," she said. "In fact, you're going to be doing giants by the time we finish bars today. I'll spot you."

I stood my ground, not mounting the bar, and Nicole was losing patience. "You know what, Simone?" she said. "You're doing a giant right now."

"You can't make me!" I said, crying harder.

Nicole reached over and easily lifted my skinny eight-year-old frame, then placed my hands on the bar. At this point, I was sobbing so hard I couldn't see anything.

"I can't, I can't—" I wailed.

"You can," Nicole said firmly as she spun me up into a handstand. She held my legs straight up with one hand and held onto my arm with the other, and then she spun me around the bar. Then she did it again. And again. The whole time, she just kept spinning me around the bar, keeping her hands on my arm so I wouldn't fall. *I'm going to die!* I kept thinking. *I can't do this!* But while the voice in my head said one thing, my motions were proving that I *could* do a giant.

After a while, I calmed down enough to get the feel of the rotations, and I began to pay attention to my form, fully stretching out my legs and pointing my toes, trying to make my shape like a perfectly straight spoke in a wheel. When

Nicole finally let me dismount, my fear was gone. But it had been replaced by another emotion: anger at being forced to get back up on the bar before I'd felt ready.

I glared at Nicole. But she was hardcore. "See?" she said. "You're just fine, Simone."

I stormed off to the bathroom without another word. I knew if I'd stayed out there I'd be tempted to say something rude, and my parents would never let me get away with that. Later, though, I had to admit that Nicole had done me a favor. As scared and angry as I was, she'd refused to let me psych myself out. She helped me see that even after an ugly fall from the high bar, a giant was nothing I couldn't handle.

Nicole was on the sidelines the following January as I performed flawless giants as part of my level six bar routine. I'm sure she must've been secretly pleased that she'd pushed me beyond my comfort zone that day, because I easily passed the test and immediately began learning the skills for level seven.

At that point, Aimee took over as my main coach. She was in charge of training Bannon's team gymnasts from level seven and up. My coaches had been eager to get me to level seven, because that's when JO gymnasts finally get to add their own optional routines, pushing the degree of difficulty on required skills and looking toward larger state and regional meets. But I wasn't thinking that far ahead, at least not yet. Maybe that's why I ended up having to take the level seven test twice. The first time I kept falling off the bars, mixing up my skills on the beam, and doing little hops on landing from my tumbling passes on the floor. The second time, I performed much better, sticking all my landings and not wobbling or messing up on the beam.

The difference? I'd practiced so much that I knew the skills cold, which meant I could go out on the floor and just enjoy the feeling of flying, bouncing, and whirling through air; I could just have fun. I'd put in the hours to polish my form, fully extending my limbs for a long, clean, graceful line. Most important, my mind was in the game—I was determined not to fail level seven a second time. I'm not sure what was going on with me the first time, except I've noticed that, sometimes, when we're zooming along and it's all blue skies, we can suddenly hit a bump in the road. That's tough, but it can also force us to slow down and reassess what we want, where we're going—and just how hard we might need to work to get there.

———

While some gymnastics skills came fairly easily to me, it was clear from the start I'd have to put in a lot of extra effort on bars. I didn't love that apparatus the way I loved all the others, and at first my instinct was to avoid it. Aimee explained bars were harder for me because I was so short and my hands were small. That's why the jump to the regulation height high bar felt like a crazy daredevil move. Not gonna lie: the only thing I've ever been truly afraid of in gymnastics—apart from letting everyone down—was that high bar.

Bars can also be tougher for a power gymnast, which I

definitely was, because power gymnasts are used to controlling the apparatus instead of letting it control them. I would drive hard through my other routines, exploding off the apparatus and gaining enough air to do multiple sequences of flips and twists. But bars were another story. I had to be willing to let the bar swing me around. I had to find the flow and get in sync with the bar, and I had to let it control me.

"I'm just not good at bars," I complained to Aimee one day. "Maybe I can just be a three-event specialist like Alicia Sacramone." Alicia was one of the gymnasts I'd read about in *USA Gymnastics* and *Sports Illustrated for Kids*. She was a beast on beam, vault, and floor, and she'd brought home numerous medals in all three. But she never touched the uneven bars.

Aimee wasn't hearing it. "You might not feel as sure of yourself on bars as you do in your other events, but you can still do a great bar routine," she assured me. Then she added, "You have the ability to go as far as you can dream, Simone. You're good enough to be a champion all-around gymnast, but you're going to need to master all four events to get there."

After that, Aimee worked hard to build my confidence on bars. We'd practice the routines till I was dreaming about them in my sleep. I remember when she was teaching me how to do a move called the counter swing, aka a straddle back, which is when I swing on the high bar backward with legs straddled, then let go of the high bar and catch the low bar as I'm swinging back around. When I'm doing the move,

I can't really see the low bar except through my legs, but at first I kept not looking for the low bar because it seemed so terrifyingly far away.

"Look for the bar!" Aimee kept yelling, because she could see I was flying blind.

"I don't want to look!" I yelled back. "It's too scary! I just want to swing and catch it!"

I eventually mastered the counter swing and made it through to level eight. A few months later, I tested up to level nine. I was one of only two gymnasts on Bannon's team at that level, and the only one already training on skills for level ten. At that point, Aimee and I were learning everything together, because Aimee, once a JO gymnast herself, had stopped competing at level eight. She'd wanted to continue, but she'd broken one leg so badly that she couldn't go on.

Injuries aside, in Aimee's experience the only girls who continued past level eight were those who wanted to pursue an elite career. The sport demands so much more of you after level eight: the skills get harder, and I would have to devote a lot more time. By the time I reached level eight, I was spending three or four hours at the gym every day after school. By then Adria had returned to gymnastics and was putting in hours at the gym too. I loved looking across the room during practices and seeing my sister doing her own routines.

During my level nine competition season, I was eleven years old and a sixth grader at Strack Intermediate, a public middle school that my friends Marissa and Becca also attended. Even though I was starting to win more consistently at gymnastics meets, at school I was nothing special. Okay, I was a dork. In one photo from that year, I'm rocking bell-bottom jeans with white flowers embroidered on them and a blue polo shirt. And I have on this blue macramé belt that, when I tied it around my waist, had ends hanging almost to the floor. I look at that picture now and I don't know what I was thinking. To make matters worse, I was starting to become self-conscious about my muscles, so I always wore an athletic jacket on top of whatever outfit I'd put together. I definitely wasn't one of the cool kids. Maybe the only cool thing I did in middle school was fight my way into the boys' soccer games.

"Get off the field! No girls allowed!" the boys would shout at Megan and me when we tried to get in on their game. Megan was the other girl in my class who wanted to play soccer. The boys thought we weren't tough enough to play with them, so when we tackled them for the ball, they'd kick our shins hard enough to hurt, thinking that would scare us away. But Megan and I were determined. Remember that stubborn streak I shared with my Grandma Caye? I was like, *If you're going to kick our shins, we're going to kick your shins too, and we're going to take the ball away from you.* When the boys saw how tough Megan and I were, they backed down. We ended up playing soccer with them for the entire year.

Meanwhile at meets, my hard work in the gym was starting to pay off. Even though I was now competing in local and state meets against gymnasts who were much older and taller than me, I was starting to win medals regularly. Some of the other coaches worried that I was moving too quickly and would get burned out. "Don't let her win too fast," they'd say, but Aimee didn't see any reason to hold me back. As long as I was having fun out there and not getting too stressed, she was happy to let me compete as much as I wanted.

My mom and dad were on the same page as Aimee. My family supported my gymnastics, cheering me on at meets both at home and away. And now that I was winning more, they began paying closer attention. "Simone," Mom said, hugging me after I'd earned the all-around highest score at the 2008 South Padre Invitational meet. "God truly gave you a gift."

Yet I never felt as if my parents were forcing me to keep going. Leveling up in the JO program was completely my choice. In fact, while a lot of other moms came to watch their kids during practice, my mom was never a gym mom in that way. Of course I'd have loved looking up to see her in the viewing area as I trained, but I also enjoyed the feeling that my gymnastics practice was completely my own. I found few things more exhilarating than flying high above an apparatus, tumbling through air, then landing cleanly on the dismount. There was nothing in me that wanted to stop. In fact, I was already dreaming of performing as an elite-level gymnast and making the national team. And although the 2012 Olympics were still four years away, I secretly fantasized about going with the team to London.

But I had a problem.

"My birthday is on March 14, so I will only be fifteen the year of 2012," I wrote in a five-subject notebook that I'd turned into a diary. My coach had explained that to compete in the Olympics, I'd have to turn sixteen within the Olympic year. "I won't turn sixteen until 2013, then I will have to wait a long time," I continued in my diary.

I knew that many gymnasts got injured, had already peaked, or simply lost the motivation to compete by age nineteen, which was how old I'd be when the next Olympics rolled around. There was no way to tell what my story would be eight years into the future. "I don't know if I will make it," I scribbled. Feeling deflated, I closed the notebook and rested it on my nightstand. I switched off the lamp and turned over to go to sleep.

After staring into the dark for a few minutes, I switched back on the light, picked up the notebook, and wrote one more sentence: "I want to go the farthest I can." Looking back now, that was the most important sentence I've ever written.

CHAPTER 8

—·—

Daydreamer

*"Dreams come in a size too big
so we can grow into them."*

—Josie Bissett, actress

"S imone, are you ready to do this?" Dad asked me, his gaze holding mine. He was sitting at the dining table with his laptop open, sorting through school forms and gymnastics permissions slips for Adria and me. He'd called me downstairs to fill out an entry form for an upcoming regional meet. We both knew I'd need to earn a minimum score of 34 in that statewide competition if I hoped to qualify for level nine Western Championships, which would be held a few weeks later in May 2008.

Did I mention that this competition was a big deal? Huge, actually. All the top USAG officials would be there to scout talent, including national team coordinator Martha Karolyi. If a gymnast performed well enough, Martha just might notice her and invite her to developmental camp at the world-famous gymnastics training center she and her husband, Bela Karolyi, operate in Huntsville, Texas. In gymnastics circles, it is known simply as "the ranch."

But as much as I'd daydreamed about attending gymnastics camp with some of my elite-level idols, I had something else on my mind that afternoon.

"Dad," I said, "why can't we get a dog?"

"Oh, Simone, not again," he said. "We've been over this so many times."

That was true. Adria and I had been pleading with him for a dog for years. We would ask for a puppy for every single holiday, until one Christmas we found two huge stuffed animals under the tree, one for Adria and one for me. Those things were bigger than I was! "Well, I got you your dogs," Dad said, smiling as if he was very pleased with himself. But if he thought that would make us give up asking for a real, live dog, he was wrong. And now, I had a new way to persuade him: My sister and I loved playing with our neighbor's dog, Bo. A few weeks before, our neighbor had had to travel for business, and he'd asked our parents if Adria and I would feed, walk, and play with Bo while he was gone.

"Look how well we took care of Bo," I said now. "See, Dad? That proves we'd be really responsible if we got a dog."

Dad paused over his paperwork, tapping the table with

his pen. My heart raced a little, because this was the first time he looked as if he was actually considering our request.

"Okay, Simone," he said finally. "I'll tell you what. You qualify for Westerns this year, and you'll get your dog."

"Are you serious?" I said, jumping out of my chair. I wasn't sure I was hearing him right.

"But it has to be a German shepherd," Dad added. Adria and I had always imagined getting a little dog, like a Yorkie or a Chihuahua, but if my dad was set on a German shepherd, that was fine by me. "If you train them right, they're protective, obedient, and playful," Dad told me. He then mentioned a farm named Heidelberg where they raised German shepherds. "You score high enough at regionals," he said, turning back to his paperwork, "I'll take you there to pick out a dog myself."

With motivation like that, you can bet I hit all my routines at the Region 3 Championships that spring, placing first on floor and second all-around, and qualifying for Westerns. Adria was sitting in the stands with Mom and Dad when she saw my final score of 38.100 light up the scoreboard. My sister started bouncing up and down and screaming, "We're getting a dog! We're getting a dog!" I could hear her from all the way down on the floor of the arena. What I didn't hear was when Dad groaned, looked at Mom, and said, "Oh man, now we have to get a dog."

A few months later, when school let out for the summer, Mom and Dad took us to Heidelberg to look at the stalls and stalls of puppies. Some were still too young to leave the farm, so Adria and I picked out a brown one that was old enough to go home with us right away. After pleading for so long to get a dog, we didn't want to wait even one more day. But then my mom stopped by the very last cage, where a playful little black-and-brown puppy caught her eye.

"What about that one?" she said, calling us over.

"It's not old enough yet," I said. But one of the farm workers was already pulling the puppy out of the pen and placing her in my arms. She was a frisky little thing, kind of like me, and when she began licking my face I fell in love with her right away.

"We'll come and play with her on weekends till she can come home with us," Dad promised. "It will only be a month."

"Okay, this one," I agreed. "But since I won her, I get to pick her name."

And that's how Maggie Elena Biles, German shepherd, joined our family.

Borinnnnng year!
Put it at that

I wrote that in my diary about my entire seventh grade year. My social situation at Strack Intermediate hadn't improved one bit since sixth grade. At school, there were the jocks, the cheerleaders, and the popular kids—and then there were the nobodies like me. Don't get me wrong, I had friends, and I'd get loud and crazy with them sometimes.

So many things made me crack up that I was always bursting into laughter in class. The teacher would say, "Be quiet, Simone." I wasn't ever a discipline problem, but I wasn't a shy girl either—except when I liked a boy.

There was this one boy, Dillon, who sat behind me in social studies. He had long dark hair in a Justin Bieber kind of cut. I thought he was cute. He was always whispering and joking with me in class, so I suspected he might like me too. The other kids would ask, "Are you guys gonna date?" and we'd always say no, because in seventh grade, you never admit to that. One day in class, Dillon passed a note to me that said, "Be my girlfriend." Feeling suddenly flustered, I quickly scrawled "Yes" on the note and passed it back, but after class I ran out of the room before he could say anything.

When I got to school the next morning, I didn't know how to act. So many questions swirled in my head: *Is Dillon really my boyfriend now? What does that mean? Should I go by his locker before class? What do kids do when they're dating?* I didn't have the first clue, and I didn't want to seem stupid, so when I saw Dillon in social studies later that day I called the whole thing off. "So, um, Dillon, we're not dating," I said, trying to act all casual. He just shrugged, and that was that. You could say my biggest adventure in seventh grade was having a boyfriend for one day.

The whole year, I couldn't shake the feeling that I was just passing time. That's because my parents had told us that we'd be moving soon to a larger home, a brand-new Tuscan-style house with a huge yard and a saltwater pool. I didn't know whether to be excited or sad about the move. On the one hand, Adria and I would have our own rooms that we could decorate in any way that we wanted, but on the other, I'd be leaving behind friends and starting at a new school. Worst of all, I'd miss the eighth grade dance, which all the seventh graders were already gearing up for. And since the new house was forty-five minutes farther away from Bannon's than our old one, getting to and from gymnastics practice was going to be more complicated.

I'd gotten used to carpooling to the gym with Loren from down the street. Because my mom and dad were so busy working and getting the new house ready for our move, they'd arranged for Loren's mom to pick us up at school every day, drive us to practice, and then bring us home. Loren was small and skinny with short blond hair. She was as hyper as I was and super flexible as a gymnast, and her playful antics during practice made me laugh. We were starting to become friends, but once we weren't carpooling anymore, we'd probably lose touch.

Trying to sort out my feelings about my so-called boring life, I spent my free time stretched out on my bed, making lists in my notebook: countries I'd traveled to (Belize, Jamaica, Mexico, Canada, Cayman Islands, Isla Roatan); apps I wanted for my iPod (Facebook, MySpace, Cool Facts, Moron Test, Weird Laws, Pandora, Doodle Buddy); websites to find music for floor routines (floorexpressmusic. com, goody.good); favorite TV shows (*Pretty Little Liars, Full House*); things I wanted for Christmas (digital camera, jewelry box, bedroom walls painted purple); and inspiring gymnastics quotes (Nadia Comaneci: "Jump off the beam, flip off the bars, follow your dreams and reach for the stars.").

I also spent hours planning what my bedroom at the new house would look like (zebra-print comforter, purple Phoebe lamp, wooden letters spelling out *Simone*, trophy case, tie-dye bulletin board, zebra bean bag) and designing my own line of leos. I daydreamed about who would recruit me for college gymnastics (LSU, University of Alabama, UCLA, Ohio State) and even planned my future wedding down to the smallest details (carriage pulled by white horses, lilacs and purple orchids, heart-top dress, edible arrangements, releasing doves, honeymoon in Bora-Bora).

Oh, there was also a list of 100 Things to Do After 2016 (cliff jumping, snowboarding, skydiving, swim with sharks, ride elephants, swim with dolphins). In that last list was a clue that I was already starting to look ahead toward the 2016 Olympics, because I didn't plan to do anything before then that might cause me to get injured. Then again, since I was now competing at level ten and had recently told Aimee and my parents I definitely wanted to go elite, I needed to ramp up my weekly training schedule, so where would I find the time for cliff jumping anyway?

Aimee and my mom were trying to figure out how I could fit in more hours at the gym even though I would now be living farther away. Aimee offered to pick me up and drive me to practices herself, but in the end, my parents found another solution. They enrolled me in a private middle school that was right across the street from the gym; the plan was for me to finish seventh grade and do eighth grade there. This would allow me to add two hours of train-ing every morning, from seven to nine a.m., and then I could just walk across the street to school. In the afternoon, I'd simply walk back to the gym for my second training session of the day. This would increase my gym time from twenty to thirty hours a week—and that was the good news.

The bad news? I hated my new school.

———

"Somalia, please answer the question."

It was my second day at private school, and I didn't know the other students' names yet, so I looked around to see who one of my teachers had called on. I was glad it wasn't me, because this man's voice was such a slow, monotonous drawl that I'd spent the entire class trying not to fall asleep. I hadn't even heard the question. When no one spoke up, I looked back at the teacher and realized he was staring straight at me.

"Somalia?" he said. "We're waiting."

A girl next to me whispered, "That's you! He's talking to you!"

I cleared my throat and started to explain my name was Simone, but before I could speak, the teacher decided I didn't know the answer and he called on somebody else. That teacher never did get my name right. He called me Somalia for a whole year, maybe because there was a map of Somalia on the wall behind my head. Some kids told me later he had diabetes and that was why his energy was so low. More than once, he actually fell asleep in the middle of a sentence. I'm not even kidding. He'd be reading a lesson, droning out every word, and then nothing. Just silence. The weird thing was the kids in my class didn't even think it was funny. They'd just sit there quietly, waiting for him to wake up and keep going.

I figured out pretty quickly that a lot of the kids at my new school had learning challenges or behavior issues, which is why the classes were kept small. In eighth grade, only seven students were in my homeroom—and one of them tried to stab me.

Brandon (not his real name) had something a little bit wrong with him. He hated getting any grade below a ninety. Whenever he scored lower than that, he'd dig his pencil into his arm, dragging it back and forth until he saw blood.

One day, he got back an eighty-one on a test right at the end of class. I was sitting next to him that afternoon, and as he took up his pencil, I grabbed it away.

"Brandon, don't do that, please," I said. The way he cut himself scared me. But what I didn't realize was that Brandon had a pocketknife, so I wasn't prepared when he pulled it out and tried to stab my hand. Luckily, he missed, and I didn't wait for him to try again. I jumped up from my seat and ran out of the classroom without waiting for the teacher to dismiss us. Brandon ran after me, waving the pocketknife, but I was faster than he was. I raced outside the building and jumped over a gate that led to another part of the school, and I padlocked the gate behind me. I heard Brandon banging and pushing at the gate, trying to get it open, but I didn't look back. I just kept running until I got to the safety of the school office.

"B-B-Brandon is trying to stab me!" I yelled. I barely got the words out, I was so terrified. The woman at the front desk was totally calm. She said, "Oh, we've known Brandon since the first grade, and he would never do that."

Seriously?!

My parents were pretty upset when I told them what happened. They went in and talked to my teachers, who made sure to separate me from Brandon for the rest of the year. Since we all knew I wouldn't be at that place for much longer, they let it go at that. I couldn't wait to be reunited with my public school friends in high school.

———※———

The gym became my refuge. I wished I could spend my days there, instead of going to the private school between my morning and afternoon sessions. Even though I was the only team gymnast training at level ten, I had made some good friends at Bannon's, including two girls who are my BFFs to this day.

One was Caitlyn Cramer, who came to Bannon's to try out for JO gymnastics classes when we were both nine years old. I remember the year because I turned ten shortly after, and as soon as I did, Caitlyn dubbed me the "double digit midget." She had the whole gym calling me that. She was a lot taller than I was, with dark brown hair and big dark brown eyes. She looked a little bit like one of my idols, Shawn

Johnson, who had won the 2006 US Junior National All-Around Championship with a score that was higher than all her senior-level competitors.

Caitlyn's first day at Bannon's happened to fall on stair day, which meant we'd spend an hour running up and down the gym's two levels of stairs.

"Oh man," I told her, "you picked the wrong day to try out."

She laughed nervously and told me her name. She said her family had just moved to Houston from Ohio.

"I was born there!" I said, bonding with the new girl over our Buckeye State connection.

Sure enough, by the end of cardio conditioning we felt like we were dying. "OMG! You were right!" Caitlyn gasped. She was hunched over and breathing hard with her hands on her knees. But when her mom came to pick her up at the end of class, Caitlyn said she definitely wanted to stay at Bannon's. Later, she told me it was because of me.

My other bestie at Bannon's was Rachel Moore. She started out in Adria's group, but she was my age and we had a lot in common. She had short hair like me, and we went to the same Dominican hair stylist for a while. Some Saturdays, we'd make appointments together so we could hang out at the hair salon as well as at the gym. Rachel was generally a happy person to be around. At Bannon's, if I started getting really hyper, Rachel was the one who'd settle me down and tell me to focus. And she and her mom often drove hundreds of miles to cheer me on at gymnastics competitions.

I was doing fairly well in most of my meets, but until I

began competing at levels nine and ten, no one paid much attention to individual wins. We were competing for the glory of our team, and all the major accolades went to our gyms. But at level ten, that began to change, because most gymnasts at that level were intending to pursue an elite career. The USAG began tracking these higher-level gymnasts more closely to see who might show potential for future national and international assignments.

The first big level ten win I remember was at the Houston National Invitational in 2010. Out of 652 gymnasts competing, I placed first on vault and floor, and third all-around, and at the end I was presented with a huge cardboard check for $5,000. That check was as tall as I was, and when they brought it over, Aimee stepped in and took it. "Let me hold this for you," she said. "You can't touch the check or you'll be NCAA ineligible." She explained that my winnings would have to go to my gym program instead of to me as an individual, because once athletes accepted money for their performance, it meant they'd turned pro and could not compete in college.

Aimee knew I looked forward to the day when I could compete in NCAA gymnastics for a top college team, but she didn't realize how literally I'd taken her explanation. I didn't want to do *anything* that would jeopardize my chances of being a college gymnast, so later that day when the press photographer wanted to take a picture of me holding the big cardboard check, I kept telling him, "I can't touch it!" He was so confused. One of the meet organizers tried to simply lean the check against me for the pictures, but I jumped out of the way.

"Simone, please, you have to pick up the check," the photographer pleaded.

"No, no, my coach said don't touch it," I said, looking around for Aimee, who, at that moment, was nowhere to be seen.

Finally, my dad came over. "Simone," he said, "this is just a copy of the real check. You *can* touch it. You just can't accept the real thing."

I was like, "Oh."

How embarrassing.

After the Houston National Invitational, Aimee sent a video of my routines to Martha Karolyi. Aimee was hoping I'd get an invitation to attend developmental camp at Karolyi's training center in Huntsville—a critical step in an elite career. But Martha's response wasn't encouraging. "This kid has no bars," she told Aimee later. "I can't let her come to camp. She can tumble great, but that's it."

When my mom heard what Martha had said, she sat down with my coach.

"Aimee, we need to talk," she said. "I know you've never trained an elite gymnast. The highest you've gone at Bannon's is level ten. So I need to know whether you can take Simone farther, or do I have to find her another gym?"

"I can definitely take Simone to the elite level," Aimee told my mom.

But Momma Biles wanted to be sure. "So how are you

going to do this?" she pressed. "Do you know the skills she needs? Because I'm not going to mince words here, Aimee. You're a rookie at the elite level. But we all started out on this journey together, so if you think you're up to the challenge, then I'll take a chance and put my daughter in your hands."

Aimee promised my mom that if I ever needed more than she could give me, she'd bring in help from other coaches, and even take me to train at other gyms. So my parents decided to keep me with Aimee, which was the best thing they could have done. Aimee and I had formed a strong bond over the years. She felt like family to me. She knew where I was confident and where I was less sure, and she believed in me. Most important of all, I trusted her.

For the rest of the season, Aimee worked with me to strengthen my performance on bars and to push my degree of difficulty and consistency in all my routines. Aimee also wanted me to have fun. She knew I loved gymnastics, and she didn't want that to ever change. Before meets, she'd say, "Okay, Simone, go out there and enjoy yourself. All of those expectations people put on you, that's their baggage. It's not yours to carry. You go out there and be yourself. Do your best and don't worry about the rest."

And you know what? Her encouragement seemed to be working. At the Region 3 Championships that year, I finished fourth all-around and first on vault, which qualified me for JO Nationals in Dallas, Texas. After winning third all-around and first on floor at Nationals, I was super excited to end the season as the US Challenge Pre-Elite All-Around

Champion for 2010. At the medal ceremony, Aimee was beaming. She didn't have a single doubt that it was just a matter of time before Martha Karolyi would change her mind about me.

CHAPTER 9

Bar Release

"Courage doesn't always roar. Sometimes it's the quiet voice at the end of the day whispering, 'I will try again tomorrow.'"

—MARY ANNE RADMACHER, AUTHOR

I love Sundays. That's when I get to leave my gym clothes in the closet and put on a dress and heels for church with my family. When we come home, Adria and I will change into shorts and race around the house with our four German shepherds, whose doggie beds are lined up in the hallway right outside my bedroom door. There's Maggie, the dog we got after my level nine Westerns, and then there are her puppies Lily, Atlas, and Bella, who were bred at the same farm where we found Maggie. It's great having four big, frisky German shepherds around; we've come such a long way since the days when Adria and I had to beg our dad for just one dog. Eventually, when I get tired of playing, I'll go to my room and laze around for hours on my zebra-print comforter, flipping through gymnastics magazines as the delicious aroma of dinner fills the house.

As long as I can remember, I've devoured stories of gymnasts who travel and compete internationally as part of the USA women's national team. And in the gym, I'd press Aimee to teach me more of the tricky, high-start-value combinations that might one day land me on the same podium as the top elite girls in my sport. *How can I get where they are?* I wondered obsessively. *What skills do they have that I don't?*

I knew that performing high-degree-of-difficulty routines was the key to taking my gymnastics to the next level, especially under the revised international Code of Points introduced in 2006. That year, the old ten-point maximum score was replaced with a system that rewards each routine's difficulty and technical content (the D score), as well as the gymnast's execution and artistry (the E score). The D score has no upper limit, while the E score tops out at ten points. Both numbers are tallied for the final event score, with anything above fifteen points usually in medal range. All of this meant that the sooner I could do the hard skills flawlessly, the greater my chance of climbing onto the winner's podium.

On Valentine's Day 2011, I finally got the chance to

compete using some of my new skills while at the Gliders National Elite Qualifier in Riverside, California. There I was, the pint-sized, muscled girl in the swirly black-and-pearl-white leo, my hair neatly cornrowed into a topknot. At four feet eight inches tall, I looked about ten years old even though I'd turn fourteen in exactly one month.

As I stood at the end of the vault runway, waiting for the signal to perform my optional vault, I felt jittery with anticipation. Time seemed to crawl, as if all the action around me was happening in slow motion.

Earlier, my compulsory vault had gone well enough, but I'd taken a small step on the landing, and I wanted my second vault to be flawless. Finally, the judge raised the start flag. I lifted both arms above my head, flashed a smile in the usual salute to the judges, then stepped to the center of the runway. The sounds in the gym faded to a hush, until all I was aware of was the runway and the vault table at the end of it. Adrenaline coursed through me as I visualized just how I'd hit the springboard. I imagined the sound of my hands punching off it, and the feel of my body lifting, spinning weightlessly through the air before surrendering to gravity, my feet finding the mat. I took a deep breath and sprinted toward the vault, hitting my round-off back handspring entry cleanly and soaring high off the table into a double twist, then falling to earth on the layout, digging my toes into the bright blue padding and lifting my chest to stick the landing.

"Nice job!" Aimee said, high-fiving me as I stepped off the mat. There was no time to analyze the vault like we did in practice. Aimee put a hand on my back and steered me over to the uneven bars for my next event. All around us, other gymnasts were performing their routines, and officials with clipboards were tracking them. I did just okay on the uneven bars. My routine was pretty basic, and my execution wasn't as smooth as it could have been—definitely not enough to push me to a win. Next up was the balance beam: I wobbled a bit but made it through the entire event without falling, and even put together a back handspring, and then a one-arm back handspring, followed by a two-and-a-half twist off the beam.

Floor has always been my favorite event. Aimee told me later that as I launched into my first tumbling pass, people who were milling around and chatting suddenly became still, watching me. "Wow, she can really tumble," somebody said.

When final scores were posted at the end of the meet, I emerged as vault champion and—seemingly out of nowhere—I'd taken first place all-around. This was my debut as a junior elite gymnast, and somehow I'd managed to win gold right out the gate! A part of me felt as if the result was a fluke, but another part of me was starting to believe I really could go all the way to Nationals—*and* make the 2011 women's junior team.

With the win at Gliders, that goal seemed within reach, because my score had qualified me to compete in the American Classic at the Karolyi Ranch on July 1. Anyone who did well enough at that meet would automatically go on to compete at the Visa National Championships in August. *That* was the golden ticket, because Martha Karolyi would select the next artistic gymnastics women's senior and junior national teams based on the results at Nationals. My entire plan now was to be one of the chosen.

———

I'm always surprised when people say I was a late bloomer, because gymnastics has been my life since I was six years old. What they really mean is that, until I was fourteen, I wasn't on anybody's radar. I'd never been invited to gymnastics camp at Bela and Martha Karolyi's sprawling ranch in Huntsville, which meant I hadn't been identified as a possible candidate for a spot on the USAG's national team.

All that was about to change. When Aimee sent recordings of my performances to Martha the second time, Martha invited me to developmental camp at the ranch. Martha did wonder if, at fourteen, I was already too old to groom, but I guess she thought I was promising enough to at least evaluate me. I was excited and nervous.

Everyone knew that Bela and Martha were responsible for numerous Olympic and World champions, including Romanian gymnast Nadia Comaneci, who made history with her perfect tens at the 1976 Summer Games in Montreal, Québec, and American Mary Lou Retton, who took gold at the 1984 Summer Olympics in Los Angeles, California. I also knew that the women's national team members went to camp at the ranch every four to six weeks for skills training and assessments, known as verifications. I didn't know if I'd actually meet any of the girls on the team, but at least I'd be working out with a new crop of gymnasts who were up and coming like me.

Aimee drove with me to Huntsville. All the gymnasts' regular coaches also attended the five-day camp, working with Martha's staff to help push us to the next level. The Karolyi Ranch, which since 2000 has been the official training center for the USAG women's teams, is a 2,000-acre spread in the middle of a national forest. The landscape is lush and green, with a huge lake at the center, and nothing but trees and woods for miles around. Tucked in the middle of the forest are three training gyms, a dance studio, medical facilities, dining and recreational spaces, and cabins that can sleep up to three hundred athletes and coaches at a time.

As Aimee and I drove down a long, wooded road to the corrugated metal main building, I have to admit I was picturing roasting marshmallows over a campfire, movie nights with popcorn, pool time with new friends, and outdoor games designed to help campers bond. The problem was I'd taken the word *camp* to heart. I thought the week would be fun and games with some workout sessions thrown in. Boy, was I mistaken! The only bonding our coaches intended on us doing was with the vault table, the uneven bars, the balance beam, and the training floor.

Developmental camp at the Karolyi Ranch is all about raising your game. You're in the gym from eight in the morning until seven at night, with a three-hour break in between. The main gym looks like any training center, with coaches for each of the events who drill you on your skills. I was accustomed to repetition in practice, but the atmosphere was more hard-core than I was used to at Bannon's. At the ranch, coaches would help you break down each skill into its basic elements so you could improve every part of the routine.

Martha would walk around from station to station, observing everything and making comments to our coaches. I don't remember actually speaking to Martha at that first camp, although sometimes at the end of practice she'd line us up—always in height order—and give us little pep talks in her thick Eastern European accent. "We strive for perfection here," she told us. "If that's not your goal, then you're in the wrong place."

First-timers at the ranch are always a little intimidated by Martha. She's very no-nonsense, and she wants results fast. If she thinks you're not giving one hundred percent, she'll say, "Well, you're not doing this for me, you're doing it for yourself." But she's always there to help you set goals and achieve them. She'll push you to limits that you don't think you can reach, and yet somehow you do. She definitely wants you to be your best, so I knew that everything we were doing at camp was going to make me better. But I wasn't used to such a serious environment. Even when hard practices made me cry at Bannon's, some other part of that session would make me break into laughter. It's just who I am. But I had to keep that side of me tamped down because laughter in the gym would've been seen as a sign that I wasn't committed. At the ranch, being committed meant you kept a straight face and did the conditioning drills and worked at perfecting your skills until you thought you were so tired you couldn't go on—and then you worked some more.

Let's just say that with all that formality and rigor, I was *not* a happy camper. Maybe the feeling of wanting everything to be more fun was normal for a fourteen-year-old, but there was no place for me to express that during the training. Aimee knew I was struggling; she'd caught me rolling my eyes once or twice at having to repeat a particular move again and again. The repetition was so relentless that, instead of feeling sharper, I was actually starting to feel blurry and a little bored—which might be why I started wobbling on my beam routine.

"Get it together, Simone," Aimee warned me in a low voice. She told me later that Martha had said to her, "Simone floats like a butterfly, but she has to stop falling on beam."

I was glad I had Aimee quietly in my corner. She knew better than anyone how to manage me when I became unfocused. Sometimes, depending on how she read my mood, we'd power through. Other times, when my resistance hardened into opposition, she'd send me to do conditioning and we'd tackle the skill again later.

"I would rather you do three hours of conditioning than for you to do poor technique on your gymnastics," she'd say. "I will not allow you to do bad gymnastics, because that's just a waste of time."

Fortunately, my parents had raised me to be polite even when I secretly had an attitude, so even though I wasn't enjoying the drills, I didn't dare let anyone else see that. It was not just a privilege, but also a rite of passage simply to be invited to the ranch, so I dug deeply and did everything the coaches asked. I was starting to realize that if I truly wanted to move to the next level, I was going to have to get used to this intensive style of training. Up until then, gymnastics had been mostly fun and games for me; I had to start seeing it as *work* too.

About thirty girls were at camp that week, including a few I recognized from level ten and pre-elite meets. I was rooming with Courtney Collins, Nia Dennis, and Destinee Davis. We were from different states, and we struck up a friendship outside of practice. I read years later in a *TIME* magazine article that the hidden gift of the boot camp-like atmosphere at the ranch was that the girls who attended sessions together became close friends. From my own experience, I'd say that's absolutely true. On breaks, Courtney, Nia, Destinee, and I would go for walks around the ranch to see the animals: donkeys, horses, camels, chickens, and peacocks, all roaming freely on the property. Sometimes we'd play on a swing set, which was more like a tetherball machine, with rings we could swing around on. Mostly, we spent our time in the training center, breaking skills down and putting them back together again until our execution became second nature.

I came around to appreciating Martha Karolyi's results-oriented approach when I returned to the ranch a few weeks later to compete in the American Classic. I ended up taking first on vault and balance beam in my junior session, and third all-around, with a final score of 53.650. That was a full point higher than I needed in order to qualify straight to the Visa National Championship in August.

I was in!

I'd achieved my first goal. My score also allowed me to compete at the CoverGirl Classic a couple of weeks later. On the drive back to Spring after the meet, Aimee suggested that Classics would be my last chance to add some new dream skills to my competition routine before Nationals.

—————

Back at school, teachers had started talking to my parents about my lack of concentration in the classroom. It seemed that any little thing—a bird flitting by outside, footsteps in the hallway, one student whispering to another at the back of the room—was enough to distract me from what the teacher was saying. Near the end of the school year, my dad made an appointment to have me tested. Given how hyper and energetic I'd always been as a little kid, no one was entirely surprised when it turned out I had ADHD.

The funny thing was, even with ADHD, when it came to gymnastics, I could be laser focused. With my sights now set on making the junior national team, I wanted to do more, more, more. "I just got some new skills on beam, an aerial, which is a cartwheel with no hands, and a round-off double into the pit," I wrote in my journal that year. "On bars, we're working on Tkatchevs. I hope I get it on the high bar soon. I feel like every time I learn a new skill, I have accomplished something."

Bars again—the dread of my gymnastics existence. I'd been wrestling with the Tkatchev for almost a year, trying to nail the complicated release-and-catch move. In a Tkatchev, a gymnast swings around the bar like she's doing a giant, but a little bit before she gets to the top—right when her toes are just past horizontal—she releases the bar and turns her hands over so that she'll fly backward over the bar in a straddle position and then catch the bar again on the other side.

My trouble with this skill was the same old story—a bad experience had made me afraid of the move. Here's what happened: One day when one of my other coaches at Bannon's was spotting me on bars, I threw my body into the motion for the Tkatchev, getting ready to sail backward over the bar, but at the last second, I didn't release the bar. I ended up backbending on the bar, and next thing I knew, I was spinning around on my neck and flying off the apparatus.

I think I frightened Coach Tomas (not his real name) that day. He ran over to me shouting, "Simone, what are you doing? You can't do that! You have to follow through with the skill or you'll get injured."

No, I didn't get injured, but after that, I was terrified of the Tkatchev. This is where my stubbornness did me some good, however, because as much as I wanted to never attempt that release and catch again, I didn't give up. There were days when I hit the mat with every single release I did, and I never came close to catching the bar. The problem was my timing. After I released the bar, I had to know the exact moment to catch it on the way around, and I had to be precise on every single repetition. But I was all over the place. I'd reach for the bar early and crash into it, or I'd be way too late and completely miss it. Other times, I would kind of catch it, but my grip wasn't sure and I'd slip off.

On a particular afternoon when I was slipping off the bar every time I tried to catch it, I sobbed to Aimee, "I'm never going to get it!" I was crying my eyes out that day. "Aimee, this isn't working! I've been trying to do the Tkatchev for seven months now. Why can't I learn this release move?" I was so frustrated. During the forty-five-minute bar rotation, I'd try the release and catch over and over, and I'd miss, cry, miss, cry, miss, cry. And then, just before practice ended, I said to myself, *I'm going to do it this time.* And you know what? I actually did! I was so ecstatic that now I was crying from the pure joy of finally catching the bar!

I didn't feel ready to debut the skill in competition though, because I still wasn't consistently catching the bar. But Tomas argued that I should make the Tkatchev part of my uneven bar routine for the upcoming CoverGirl Classic so I could compete with it at least once before Nationals. "You can't go to Nationals without a strong Tkatchev," he insisted. Aimee agreed. So even though I was still failing regularly on the catch, I reluctantly said yes. We all knew I needed a greater degree of difficulty on my bar routine anyway, and Tomas calculated that if I could nail the Tkatchev in competition, when the rush of adrenaline often boosted a gymnast's execution, then I might gain enough confidence to perform the skill flawlessly at Nationals.

Of course, if I miss the catch and fall in the gym, my coach just picks me up and lifts me back onto the bar to finish my routine. But falling in competition is another story. The week leading up to Classics, all I could think about was how embarrassed I'd be if I ended up crashing to the mat in front of all these elite girls who could do perfect single-bar releases in their sleep. With that self-defeating thought looping in my head, I never caught the bar once that entire week. Then during the warm-up period right before the meet, guess what? I was still missing the bar on the Tkatchev.

By now you've probably figured out that I can burst into tears almost as easily as I can burst out laughing. Stress does that to me—makes me laugh or makes me cry. So just before it was time to march out onto the floor with the other competitors, I was in the bathroom crying from sheer nerves and the fear that I was about to humiliate myself. Right then, one of the girls in my group, Lexie Priessman, came into the bathroom.

I'd read about Lexie in the pages of *USA Gymnastics* magazine, and I'd followed her competitive career online. She'd made her national team debut the year before at the Nastia Liukin Supergirl Cup in Worcester, Massachusetts, where she won the all-around title. We'd met for the first time earlier that day, but I'd been too starstruck to say much. Now, seeing my tears, she came over to me.

"Hey, are you okay?" she asked.

"No," I mumbled, dabbing at my mascara with a tissue, trying to wipe away the smudges before I went out onto the arena floor. "I keep falling on the Tkatchev. During warm-ups, I didn't catch it a single time. I've tried everything, and it's not working."

Lexie stood in front of me and put her hands on my shoulders.

"First of all, stop crying," she said. "And if it helps, I used to have a lot of trouble on Tkatchevs too. This is what helped me: just let go of the bar so early that you think you're going to land on the bar. It'll feel too soon, but just go ahead and do it. Works for me every time."

"Okay," I said, willing, at that point, to try anything.

"Now let's go out there," Lexie said. "They're calling us."

I left the bathroom and walked with one of my idols into the arena to march with the rest of my competitors. I was more aware than ever that I was about to go up against some of the best in my sport, but Lexie's kindness in the bathroom had made me a little less scared. When it was time for me to do my bar routine, I looked around and saw she was smiling at me from the sidelines with both thumbs up. I thought, *Okay, just do what she said, let go of the bar a little bit earlier than you think you should,* and that's exactly what I did. And I caught the bar! In competition!

In the moment I grabbed the bar, I heard my sister Adria's voice screaming my name from somewhere in the audience, and then I caught sight of Lexie jumping up and down and cheering.

But here's the thing: I was used to falling on my Tkatchev and having my coach put me back up on the bar. Then I'd go on from there to do a good, clean routine. Now that I'd actually *caught* my Tkatchev, everything after that was just a little bit off. I realized that all along, I'd been practicing my routine *expecting to fall,* so I didn't know how to flow smoothly into my other skills. I fell on the Pak salto—a release from the high bar to the low bar, with a backward layout just before you catch the low bar—even though I'd never before fallen on the Pak. Right after my Pak salto, I fell on a toe catch from the low bar to the high bar. But at the end of the routine, I did manage to at least stick the dismount.

As I stepped off the mat, Aimee ran over and gave me a hug. Lexie rushed up to me, face beaming, and said, "Hey, you caught your Tkatchev!"

"I did!" I said, high-fiving her. "Thank you!" Everyone else was looking at us, completely puzzled. They were probably wondering, *Why on earth is she so excited? She just fell off the bars twice!* But I didn't care right then. I'd caught my Tkatchev, and I was on my way to Nationals.

One month later, it wouldn't be the Tkatchev that would put me out of contention for the USA women's junior team by just one spot—it would be that dang Amanar. Maybe if I'd spent more time practicing the vault, I might've gotten picked. But the same thing that's true in gymnastics is also true in life: You can't go back. The best you can do is forgive yourself, take a deep breath, and get to work on the next challenge. But that doesn't mean you can't bawl first—and let me tell you, I did.

CHAPTER 10

Game Change

"Sometimes not getting what you
want is a brilliant stroke of luck."

—Lorii Myers, author

I stood on the sidelines of the arena in St. Paul, Minnesota, clapping till my palms stung. The roar of the audience drowned out my own cheers for the thirteen newly selected members of the USA women's junior team. The two-day 2011 Visa National Championships were over. While I'd loved meeting so many of my idols and competing against the best my sport had to offer, the meet hadn't turned out for me the way I'd dreamed. My bright, pasted-on smile hid my bitter disappointment. Coming in at number fourteen in the rankings, I'd missed making the thirteen-woman team by a hair, but it might as well have been a mile.

As the girls who'd been chosen began walking off the stage, family and friends swarmed onto the floor to congratulate them. Cameras flashed at such a blinding rate, the entire scene seemed to be lit by strobes. Everything felt unreal in that moment, like a bad dream I couldn't wake up from. I had spent the entire competitive season with one goal in mind, to make the national team. But I'd come up short.

I managed to keep it together till I got to the safe embrace of my parents, who waded into the crowd to find me. Mom hugged me close, while Dad patted my shoulder. They could see right past my cheerful act; they knew I was devastated. I'd been determined not to act like a big baby, but once we got back to the hotel, I couldn't hold it in any longer. Oh, I cried. I threw myself across the bed and bawled.

My parents were saying all the right things to help me feel better. "It's okay, Simone. We're proud of you. You don't need to be sad about this. You have a fresh opportunity here. This is really okay."

My mom rubbed her hand in circles on my back to try to comfort me while, above my sobbing, I could hear my dad ordering room service. I hadn't eaten since early that morning, and now it was evening. They knew I was tired and hungry, and that my exhaustion was probably making everything worse. When the food came, they coaxed me to have some. I had no idea what I was eating; it was completely tasteless. When I couldn't make myself take another bite, they suggested I go take a shower and call it a day.

"Remember, Simone, you're still just a junior, and you came so close," my mom reminded me as I dragged my sorry self to the bathroom. "You'll come back and make it next year."

In the bathroom, I turned on the shower, but I didn't get undressed right away. For a long time, I sat on the edge of the bath, mentally going over the days' routines. I would later learn how to shake off these kind of setbacks in competition and get my head back in the game. But that night, I was in despair. I was sure I'd failed everyone: my parents, my coaches, my team at Bannon's, and, most of all, myself.

I heard a light knock on the door. My mom called out that my brother was on the phone from Texas and wanted to speak to me. At the time, Ron was twenty-seven. I knew that he and his fiancée, Lindsay, had been watching my performance on TV back home. I cracked open the door and took the phone.

"Ron?"

He launched right in. "Hey, girl, I saw what happened, and I know you're disappointed right now, but you're just one slot off from making the team, and that is something!" he told me. "Because you know what, Simone, you can use this as motivation to go into the gym and train even harder. Coming in at number fourteen means you're almost there! And maybe it's just not your time yet, but trust me, your day will come, because you're that good. But maybe this is your year to get better."

I was bent over my knees, still sobbing. But somehow, my brother's words were getting through to me.

"Simone," he continued, "you have to keep your chin up. You represented Bannon's so well out there."

"Thank you, Ron," I managed to whisper. "That means a lot."

My brother wasn't quite finished. "No matter what, all of us are just so proud of you, and you need to stop being so hard on yourself. So go ahead and take your shower, and when you're done, promise me, no more tears."

My shoulders still shaking, my face still wet, I promised. And when I clicked off the call, I did feel lighter, as if I'd started to put down a great weight, releasing not just the pent-up emotions of the meet, but also the accumulated expectations that I'd placed on my own shoulders ever since deciding to go elite.

———

Back in Texas, my teammates at the gym crowded around me eagerly. It turned out they were thrilled by the way I'd represented them, and since I was the first one from Bannon's ever to compete at Nationals, they wanted to hear every detail. After a while, our head coach yelled for everyone to get back to practice, and I sat down with Aimee to review the video of my routines. That's when I discovered that, as proud as my family and the girls in the gym had been of my performance, not everyone had that point of view.

Aimee had always been my main coach, but after I went elite, she sometimes brought in other coaches and specialists to help me with certain skills. One of the coaches seemed disappointed that I'd chosen not to do a skill that the powerful Martha Karolyi herself had requested. He thought I'd failed to make the national team because I'd refused to do the Amanar. He hadn't been at the meet, but he knew from Aimee that Martha had asked to see me perform it. In my heart, I knew I wasn't ready, which is why I'd done my usual double-twisting Yurchenko. Now, in our debrief, he stressed what I already knew—that the Amanar would have increased my degree of difficulty, and that would've raised my starting score, possibly enough to push me up to number thirteen in the standings.

"No wonder you didn't make the cut," he told me. He kept beating that drum: *If only you'd done the two-and-a-half. You didn't make the team because you were too scared to do the two-and-a-half.*

While he was sure I'd choked, I was absolutely convinced that if I'd gone out and done the Amanar, I would've been rolled out of that arena on a stretcher. And that would have been much worse than my little meltdown back at the hotel!

Still, I couldn't help secretly wondering if performing the Amanar—even an imperfect one—would have been my ticket onto the team. Then again, my mom and Aimee had always told me to listen to my instincts and set my own limits. Every time I replayed Nationals in my head, I knew it wasn't fear that had kept me from doing the Amanar; it was good sense. I finally decided that it had been a quiet victory for me to stand up and say, "You know what? I don't feel properly prepared to do that vault. It's not safe." That was *huge* for a girl who loved a challenge as much as I did.

Aimee had a different approach. She'd been at the meet with me, so she'd seen the pressure I'd put on myself. The first thing she said to me was, "Simone, you have to understand you're every bit as good as those other girls. Now you just have to perform as if you believe it."

As we reviewed my videos, we talked about my tendency to overthink my performance, which made me tighten up. And when I'm tight, mistakes are inevitable. I'm not in control; my nervous energy is running the show. Aimee talked to me about adding hours to my training regimen so that I could become so rock solid on all my skills, I could go out and just enjoy myself in competition.

A lot of good actually came from me failing to make the national team my first time out. For one thing, Aimee and I zeroed in on skills I needed to upgrade, not just on the vault but also on bars, beam, and floor. When we compared my videos to those of the elite gymnasts who'd scored higher than I had, it was clear that I needed to push the degree of difficulty in all my events. Of course, no matter how high my start value was, it wouldn't help unless my execution was as clean and polished as possible.

I can see now that what I mostly lacked at Nationals was maturity—and practice time in the gym. More maturity and practice would have helped me to be *cooler* in my gymnastics: I still needed to learn how to control the explosive power and soaring height of my routines so that my landings would be spot on, because every tenth of a point counted. When a gymnast does a little hop on the landing, that's an automatic one-tenth deduction. And the judges know that the bigger the hop, the less in control the gymnast is; that's why there's a greater deduction.

In the end, the most important lesson I took from the 2011 Visa National Championships was this: a person can only fail if they stop trying, if they refuse to pick themselves up and try *harder*. It would take some time, but I finally understood that I hadn't failed at that meet. I just hadn't succeeded—yet. I simply had more work to do in order to convince the gymnastics world that I could *earn* a spot on the national team. Now I was ready to do that work. But where would I fit all the extra hours I'd need to put in at the gym?

It was August by then, and I was due to enter high school in a couple of weeks. I was already training twenty-five to thirty hours a week, and I needed to put in more like thirty-five hours a week. This dilemma is the main reason a lot of top-level gymnasts make the decision to be homeschooled, but everything in me screamed *No!* at the idea. As much as I loved gymnastics and being able to soar above the arena, I was beyond excited about attending public school again with my longtime BFF Marissa. It was time for at least two of the Cheetah girls to reunite!

I'd missed Marissa and Becca after we moved away from Shady Arbor Way and I'd transferred to the private school across the street from the gym. Even though Becca was still two grades behind me, at least Marissa and I would be going to the same high school that fall. I was stoked to share this new experience with her. I kept imagining what it would be like to be back with my public school friends, going wild at football homecoming games, joining clubs, and finding dates for prom. Together, we'd figure out the high school social scene and—let's be real—we wanted to have some fashion fun too.

All summer, Marissa and I had been texting, tweeting, and Snapchatting back and forth, making elaborate plans about what outfits we'd wear on the first day of ninth grade. For me, it would be a pair of white jean shorts with a black lace peplum blouse. And after wearing my hair constantly swept back into a regulation ponytail for gymnastics, with a braid at the front, I was looking forward to trying out some looser hairstyles.

But how would I juggle my training and a busier schedule of competitions away from home? Would my public high school allow me to miss so many days of school? Would my parents? And if they did, how far behind would I fall in my classes? How would I make up the work? I wanted the best of both worlds—the thrill and the drama of high school with all my friends *and* a top-tier gymnastics career. But could I really have it all? I didn't know. What I *did* know was that not getting a spot on the national team had made me more determined to excel in elite gymnastics.

For the first time in my gymnastics career, I was facing an agonizing decision—high school with my friends, or homeschool at the gym? As I wrestled to make that choice, I entered into a phase that would become famously known in my family as "Simone's bratty period."

CHAPTER 11

New Normal

"To map out a course of action and
follow it to an end requires courage."

—Ralph Waldo Emerson, essayist and poet

A round our dinner table on most evenings, we had the same conversation over and over: high school or home school? My mother would ask, "Which way are you leaning, Simone?" I'd just shrug, roll my eyes, and stare down at my plate. I hated talking about it all the time, but I was just as mad when everyone avoided bringing it up, as if it wasn't on my mind day and night. My parents had made it clear they'd be fine with whatever I decided. One part of me wished they'd just tell me what they thought was best for me, but my mom and dad have never been that way. They knew I had to choose, and they had given me a deadline.

The new school year was just around the corner, and if I chose to go to regular high school, they needed to enroll me. "We have to make a plan," Mom told me firmly over dinner one Tuesday. "You have until Sunday to make up your mind. Time is ticking by."

She'd cooked my favorite meal of salmon and rice that evening, but I had no appetite. The problem was, I didn't see the situation the same way my parents did. As far as they were concerned, going to high school meant I'd no longer be pursuing an elite career—in my dad's words, I'd be giving up "all this gymnastics business"—but I didn't agree. Why couldn't I do both? Dad told me I was being unrealistic. "The public school system in the state of Texas won't allow you to miss as many days as you'll have to miss if you make the national team and have to go to monthly team camps and do these international assignments," he explained.

Mom chimed in. "You can always go to high school if you want," she said. "If you have your heart set on it, that's absolutely okay, but you have to know that you're also deciding to give up all this gymnastics stuff." And yes, she actually called it that—gymnastics *stuff*.

"I can do both!" I insisted, my voice rising. "Lots of girls do both!"

"Very few of the top gymnasts can manage that," my mom said, hoping her levelheadedness would calm me down.

I was in no mood to be calmed down. I'd tried hard to make peace with the idea that an elite gymnastics career would require certain sacrifices. But why did high school with my friends have to be one of them?

"You *can't* do both," my dad repeated for the umpteenth time. He sighed, looking up at the ceiling as if he was praying for God to give him strength. "Honestly, Simone, you're wearing us out with this."

"Katelyn Ohashi does both," I argued, naming the gymnast who'd taken first place at Nationals. She was just a few days younger than I was, but she'd been named to the national team two years before. I wanted to be just like her.

"She's not in Texas," Dad said.

"Yes, she is! She's in Dallas!" I knew that Katelyn trained with Nastia Liukin, the 2008 Olympic all-around gold medalist, at the World Olympic Gymnastics Academy in Plano, just outside of Dallas. I didn't mention to my dad that while I was sure that Katelyn *used to* attend public school, I wasn't so sure she was still was. It didn't matter; he wasn't buying my argument anyway.

"Okay, but she's not in *Houston*," Dad said. "Even within states, different public school districts have different rules about how many days you can miss."

That seemed just plain stupid to me. The way I figured it, if you were getting your classwork done, it didn't matter how many days of school you missed. As irritated as I was by all this, deep down I was beginning to grasp what my parents already knew: no matter which path I chose, I'd be giving up *something*. The question was, which experience did I want more—high school homecoming games and senior prom and wild, crazy times with my friends, or the international experience at gymnastics meets with the girls I'd been reading about for years?

As I weighed the question, my heart felt heavy and water filled my eyes. I thought they were tears of anger at my parents for trying to shut down my options, but looking back on it now, I can see what was really happening—I was sad that I wouldn't get to take part in an experience I'd been dreaming about for so long. I knew what I had to do, but I wasn't ready to admit it yet. And so it was easier to lash out at my parents, to make them the bad guys who were standing in my way.

"Neither of you understand me!" I cried as Adria studied the peas on her plate. I was so full of fourteen-year-old drama, you'd have thought I was auditioning for my own reality show, especially when I pushed away from the table and stood up in a huff, my chair scraping the tile of the kitchen floor.

"Sit back down, Simone," my mother said, her voice tired. But I'd recently turned into a cranky, disobedient girl, and so, with my dinner hardly touched, I ran to my room and slammed the door.

My family was becoming used to these temper tantrums. Ever since failing to make the national team, I'd been in a funky mood. Normally, Mom and Dad wouldn't have tolerated such rudeness. In this case, I think they were being more lenient than usual because they knew how much I'd wanted the social experience of high school after my lonely year in private school. I was looking forward to ordinary teenager fun like meeting up with my girls at the movies or going shopping at the mall. I was even excited about picking

▲ Simone arriving in Texas, following
her time in foster care, March 2000

Courtesy of the Biles family

▼ Simone and her sister Adria playing
dress-up, December 2000

Courtesy of the Biles family

▲ Simone and her sister Adria (center) with
their childhood friends Becca (left), one of
Simone's best friends since childhood and
fellow "Cheetah Girl," with big sister Camille
(right), also a great friend of the Biles sisters

Courtesy of the Biles family

▲ Simone hanging out with her dog Maggie, August 2009

Courtesy of the Biles family

◄ Simone and Adria head off to school, August 2007

Courtesy of the Biles family

▼ Grandma Caye in Belize during a family visit

Courtesy of the Biles family

Simone early in her career, performing a floor exercise routine at the 2011 Visa National Championship in St. Paul, Minnesota

© John Cheng

▲ Simone in her first car—complete with zebra interior—a few days after her sixteenth birthday

Courtesy of the Biles family

◀ Simone with her sister (front left), godfather (back left), godmother (back right), and mom (front right) after her confirmation

© *esmephotos.com*

◀ Celebrating Christmas with siblings Adam (far left), Adria (second to right), and Ron II (right), 2015

Courtesy of the Biles family

▶ Simone Biles at the 2016 Secret U.S. Classic at the XL Center in Hartford, Connecticut, on June 4, 2016, midflight during her bar routine

© *John Cheng*

Simone is all smiles while performing her gold-medal-winning floor routine during the event finals at the 2016 Rio Olympic Games

Lovetsky/AP/REX/Shutterstock

▲ Simone executing a near-perfect vault on August 7 during the qualifying round at the 2016 Olympic Games in Rio de Janeiro, Brazil

© John Cheng

▲ Simone Biles contributing a solid beam routine during the women's gymnastics team competition at the 2016 Olympic Games on August 9, Rio de Janeiro, Brazil

© John Cheng

▽ Simone Biles with her mother, Nellie, (far left), sister Adria (second from left), national team coordinator Martha Karolyi (second from right) and father, Ron (far right) before the start of the 2016 Rio Olympics.

© John Cheng

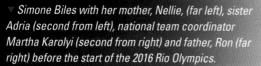

▲ The Final Five celebrating together after receiving their Olympic gold medals in team competition at the 2016 Rio Games. Pictured, left to right: Laurie Hernandez, Aly Raisman, Martha Karolyi, Simone Biles, Madison Kocian, and Gabby Douglas

© John Cheng

▼ Simone shares a high-five with her coach, Aimee Boorman, after completing a routine at the 2013 World Championship in Antwerp, Belgium

© John Cheng

out my classes and figuring out what school clubs to join. And after years of track suits and crystal-covered leos on competition days, just getting dressed every day for school seemed like an adventure I couldn't wait to start.

Sometimes, late in the evening, Mom would knock on my door. She'd come in, sit on the side of my bed, and talk to me softly. "If high school is that important to you, just go," she'd say after I'd explained yet again how much I dreamed about just being a "normal" teenager. "If it will make you stop crying and complaining about this, then just go to high school, Simone."

But the next day, after mastering some new skill in my workout with Aimee, I'd change my mind back to home-school and an elite career. Other times, when I was feeling stuck all over again about which path to take, I'd whimper, "Mom, tell me what to do." She and my dad refused to take the decision out of my hands.

My mom broke it down this way. "Simone," she said, "this won't be the only big decision you'll ever have to make, but it will most certainly be one that, when you look back, you'll see that this was a fork in the road, and you'll need to be one hundred percent okay with whatever route you decide on. That's why you have to make this decision yourself. But know that whatever you choose, we are completely behind you."

Other times, my dad would take over, laying out the pros and cons. "You can go to public school and quit elite gymnastics tomorrow if that's what you want," he'd say. "Or if it's more important to you to make the national team, to travel and compete internationally, you can do that too. Most kids don't get to do that, but you have that option. But you'd need to be homeschooled to do that. The good thing is, whether you choose public school or homeschool, you can do college gymnastics either way."

My dad knew how much I'd always wanted to compete with a top college gymnastics team like the University of Alabama or UCLA. I felt as passionate about that as I did about my goal of making the US national team. *At least I wouldn't have to give up all my dreams*, I'd think. Then Adam said something that helped me gain a sense of humor about the debate I was having with myself. "Well, sis," he said, "if you decide on homeschool, you'll be at the top of your class." He paused and then added, "But you'll also be at the bottom of your class." We all laughed, which was a nice change from me slamming doors.

It eventually occurred to me that even if I was being homeschooled, I could still see my friends in public school. We texted, tweeted, and sent Snapchats to each other all the time anyway, so really, we could stay in touch. And when I looked into it a little more, I realized that most of the girls in the elite gymnastics world were already being home-schooled. That made me feel a little better—I'd be just like the girls I'd spent so many years looking up to.

But what finally pushed me to make up my mind was something my dad had told me years before. He'd said, "Simone, never squander what God has given you." When I thought about that, I realized God had given me the abil-ity to do gymnastics in a powerful way. He'd also gifted me with a love for the sport and a passion for competing. I didn't want to waste that. Once I approached it that way, the decision seemed inevitable. Besides, if it turned out that all the extra hours I'd now be putting in at the gym didn't give me enough of an edge to make the national team next year, I could always go to the public high school for tenth grade.

The next day, I walked into my mom's home office, where she was busy working, and I announced, "Okay, Mom, I'm going to try homeschool."

"Thank God," Mom said. "And guess what? I already have the perfect teacher lined up for you."

The perfect teacher Mom had chosen turned out to be none other than my dad. He'd been researching online high school curriculums ever since the homeschool question first came up, and now he was ready. By then he'd retired from the FAA and was helping Mom run the financial side of the fourteen nursing homes she co-owned, so he simply adjusted his hours so that he could devote four of them to tutoring me in between my morning and afternoon workouts at the gym. Right from the start, it was a disaster. What teenager wants her father teaching her history and algebra? Dad thought I was a whiner and a procrastinator, which made him exasperated and annoyed. We ended up fussing at each other almost every single day.

To make matters worse, the online curriculum Dad had chosen required students to do their classwork on a certain schedule—but I was always in gym practice at those times.

Afterward, I'd come back to the computer and there'd be a million messages flashing on the screen: "Simone, where are you?" I was like, *Isn't this supposed to work with my schedule? What kind of flexibility is this?* So then they would email my assignments, and I'd breeze through them, but somehow I wasn't turning them in the right way. I didn't know that until my first progress report arrived six weeks later.

"This isn't possible!" I burst out as I stared at the single sheet of paper with my name at the top. Underneath, for every subject except Spanish, I saw F, F, F, F, F.

I was in shock, because up to then I'd always been a solid A or B student. As crushed as I was, my dad was in disbelief. "Simone, if you were struggling in all these subjects, why on earth didn't you ask for help?" he said. He just kept looking at the report card and shaking his head.

That's when my mom decided that this perfect arrangement was *not* all that perfect. Mom "fired" my dad (I think he was actually relieved), and hired a new tutor named Miss Heather to take over. Miss Heather had previously been a high school teacher and now she worked at Bannon's, home-schooling some of my teammates. She was tall and lanky with short brown hair and thin eyebrows, and she had a very patient style of teaching. I loved that her lesson plans were the same ones used for ninth grade in the public high school I would have attended. Miss Heather had all the books sent to me, and she made sure I was keeping pace with what all the public school kids in my grade were doing. Best of all, she'd been a math major in college. Since I wasn't the best math student in the world, she helped me get up to speed.

Miss Heather would come to Bannon's three days a week for four hours each day; on the other two days, I was on my own. On those days, I'd go upstairs to the break room to work for three or four hours. I had to write papers and do projects just like the public school kids, but Miss Heather's approach to testing was a little different. As long as I was understanding the lesson and moving along with the work, she'd test me at the end of each unit, rather than make me take all the chapter tests in between. She thought too many tests were a waste of valuable learning time—my kind of teacher.

If you can't already tell, I loved being tutored by Miss Heather. In her shy, soft-spoken way, she helped me feel confident about my studies, and by the next progress report, my grades had returned to normal. I stayed with Miss Heather for ninth, tenth, and eleventh grades. Later on, in twelfth grade, I worked with another great teacher my mom hired, Miss Susan. My mom, my dad, me, even Adria—we all exhaled. It seemed as if this homeschool thing was going to work out after all. Now if only I could transfer that great new attitude to my workout sessions in the gym.

CHAPTER 12

———◆———

Redemption

"The fears are paper tigers. You can do anything you decide to do."

—AMELIA EARHART, AUTHOR AND ADVENTURER

Aimee was waiting for me over by the balance beam. I strolled to where she was and dropped my grip bag onto the mat. "What's my next assignment?" I asked. I was late getting back from my mid-morning break, and we both knew it. But I was acting all casual, like it didn't even matter.

"Ten routines on beam," Aimee said, adjusting a foam mat at one end of the padded, four-inch-wide plank of suede-covered wood.

"Ten routines? That's too many!" I protested.

Aimee didn't even look in my direction. She was clearly

not happy with me. My bratty behavior had been on full display earlier that morning, when I'd resisted my conditioning workout every step of the way, muttering under my breath or talking back about why I didn't think I needed to do extra stair runs. It was true that I had a slight cold and felt a little under the weather, but Aimee wasn't cutting me any slack.

"Simone, I'm not playing around," she said now. "You have to make every connection in order for the routine to count."

"Fine!" I said, my displeasure clear in my tone.

I straightened my back, lifted my chin, and held my hands above the beam, fingers together like dance hands. I took a deep breath, mounted the beam, and launched into my first routine. Toward the end, I paused a beat too long between two back handsprings that were supposed to flow smoothly together.

"Doesn't count," Aimee said. "Start again."

All through beam practice, Aimee kept repeating that.

"No, doesn't count. You missed the connection. Start over."

I was getting aggravated because sometimes Aimee stopped me when I was sure I'd made the connection, and other times, she let a repetition go when it seemed to me that I'd been a little bit off. Finally, when I'd managed to put together seven routines that counted, I burst out, "Oh my gosh! How am I still on beam routines?"

"Well, you're making two out of three connections," Aimee told me. "You need to make all three."

"Not fair," I shot back. "The third one's a bonus connection."

"You still have to connect it," Aimee said, her voice firm. We both knew that most days she allowed the routine to count even when the bonus skill wasn't flawlessly bridged, but not today. I was confused and frustrated; I hated hearing Aimee say no to me over and over, and I also had a runny nose.

"I need to blow my nose," I said.

"Go," Aimee said, waving me off. "But then you get back on that beam and finish your routines."

"But I already did seven," I argued. That was highest number Aimee usually assigned. Most days, it was only five.

"Do three more," she said. "And connect those skills."

I felt so angry and powerless that I started crying and couldn't seem to stop. So after every dismount from a routine, whether it counted or not, I'd go off to the bathroom to blow my nose. Meanwhile, Aimee was getting more and more mad.

"Simone, if you don't get back up on this beam in ten seconds, I'm going to add another routine!" she yelled while I was still in the bathroom. At this point, I was sobbing so loudly that everyone could hear me out in the gym. Then I just lost it.

"I don't care!" I screamed. "Go ahead and add it!"

When I finally made it through the entire beam rotation, I mumbled just loud enough for Aimee to hear, "All those reps better count toward my beam workout later. And tomorrow too, because I already did eighteen routines today."

Aimee looked at me calmly and didn't say anything. When I came back later for my afternoon workout, she said, "Okay, Simone, five beam routines."

"I already did them this morning!" I insisted with an attitude.

"Doesn't matter," Aimee said pleasantly. "Give me five more."

That was one of the worst days Aimee and I ever had. And she didn't even call my parents, as she sometimes did when I was being uncooperative. Oh, and let me tell you, I hated it when she called in my parents. It usually meant a lecture from my dad about me not appreciating my opportunities, and sometimes my mom would threaten to pull me out of gymnastics altogether.

Everyone knew my dad at the gym. He would come early to pick up Adria and me so he could come inside to see what we were working on. But people hardly ever saw my mom. To tell the truth, I don't think she ever had much of a clue about my routines; she didn't even know what the big skills were called. All she knew was what she saw me perform in competition. But she preferred it that way. She thought a little distance from my gymnastics allowed us both some necessary perspective. As she always told me, "I'm not your fan, Simone; I'm your mom."

Still, whenever she did show up at Bannon's, everyone knew what that meant—something needed fixing, whether it was my attitude or something about the gym. The coaches would whisper to one another, "Look, Mrs. Biles is here." They knew my mom owned her own company and was the boss everywhere she went. She might be a short little woman with a soft manner, but she held a lot of power and authority behind that sweetly smiling face. Plus, nothing could make me feel worse than knowing I'd disappointed Momma Biles. That's why I was grateful whenever Aimee dealt with my brattiness herself and didn't call my parents.

I was now training more than thirty-five hours each week, with an intense focus on strength, conditioning, and connecting my skills to ensure that the whole routine looked effortless. I still loved the feeling of flying that I got from gymnastics—that hadn't changed—but Aimee will tell you that for almost two years my attitude sucked. Maybe in the back of my mind, I was still mad about having to give up on public school; maybe my ADHD medication needed adjustment; or maybe my teenage hormones were just raging in a completely normal way. Whatever was going on with me, it didn't help that my days were so long and my routine so regimented. Sometimes I simply didn't want to have to go through hour after hour of somebody telling me what to do.

Aimee recently described to a friend what my now famous "bratty period" looked like from her point of view: "Simone would be just kind of flinging her body around and not being committed to trying to be the best she could be," she said. "When a child is doing that, it's just about control. What she's really saying is, *I'm going to show you that I don't have to do what you say.* I know Simone's family life is very disciplined. And so when she came to the gym, it was like her time to rebel, because she wasn't going to act that way at home. At least once a week during that time, I would have either Ron or Nellie in the office, and I'd say, 'Okay, I have to let you know what happened today.' I have to say it was always effective in getting Simone back on track. What I recall is a lot of under-the-breath talking back and mumbling, but, really, she was never outwardly defiant. Besides, I work with adolescent and teenage girls every day. They're *all* bratty. Simone's brattiness, when she looks back on it now, was huge to her, but I've been coaching thirteen- and fourteen-year-old girls for years. So I'm watching not just one girl act out, but a whole group of girls doing it at the same time. And I'm like, *Go ahead, have your attitude, but do the work.* Teenage girls don't scare me."

I'm glad now that Aimee stuck by me, because I wouldn't be where I am today without her. In the elite world, everyone loves my coach because they know how understanding she is. They know she thinks that even though gymnastics is hard work, it should also be enjoyable. Otherwise, why do it? Some coaches are like, "I don't care if you're hurting, go and do that skill." And they think that if you're having fun out on the floor, it means you're not serious. Not Aimee. She carefully assesses every situation and keeps it real. Sometimes, like on the afternoon with the beam routines, she'll push me hard. But other times, she'll notice I'm exhausted and say, "Simone, it's not working today. Go home. I think you could use some rest."

⸻

Even though my emotions were on a bit of a roller coaster, that didn't mean I wasn't intensely focused on my training. By the time the next competition season began in January 2012, I felt much stronger physically than I had the previous year, and my consistency was better. I'd once again set my sights on winning a spot on the women's junior national team, and this time, I meant to succeed.

Going into the American Classic in May, I'd already

posted two all-around firsts in earlier meets, and one all-around third. Now I was once again on Martha's home turf in Huntsville. I knew I'd have to prove myself in this meet, and I was relieved when I took first place all-around for my group—and first place on vault! I confess being vault champion meant almost more to me than winning the all-around. A year before, my coaches had been convinced that not doing the two-and-a-half twist had taken me out of the running for the national team. This time, with Martha and everyone looking on, I'd killed it on the Amanar.

I'd done okay in my other events too, tying for second on floor, placing third on beam, and fourth on uneven bars. Best of all, my overall score qualified me to go straight through to the Visa National Championships at the end of the season, which put me in contention for a spot on the 2012 national women's junior team.

Just being in competition with other junior elite girls like Katelyn Ohashi and Lexie Priessman pushed me to raise my game. Once, I'd been hesitant to beat these girls because I was afraid they wouldn't like me if I did. I now understood how wrong that thinking was. Every one of us had worked for years to earn our place in the arena. Competing my hardest in all my events was the highest form of respect I could show to them *and* to myself.

Besides, as my mom always told me, "Don't ever compete against someone else, Simone. You don't go out there to beat another person. You go out there to do your very best. And if your very best means that you win that competition, that's the way it should be. If your very best means that you come in third or fourth, that's fine too. As long as you did your best. You don't go out there grudgingly and think, *Oh, I need to beat that person.* No, no, no. You go out there and be the best Simone you can be. And whatever that outcome is, we'll take it."

Being the best Simone I could be ended with me taking first place all-around at the US Secret Classic in Chicago, Illinois, in May, and third all-around at the Visa National Championships in St. Louis, Missouri, in June. At Nationals, I was also vault champion, after once again performing a strong Amanar. In fact, at every single meet I competed in for the entire 2012 season, I'd taken first place in vault with my Amanar. I'd been determined to never again be in a position of weakness when it came to the two-and-a-half, so my vault rankings felt like a comeback.

That evening at Nationals, standing on the podium next to all-around gold medalist Lexie Priessman and silver medalist Madison Desch, I could hardly believe that my dream was coming true. Later, after the arena's Jumbotron screen lit up with the names of the 2012 women's junior national team, I was smiling so hard that the muscles in my face actually ached. Perhaps because the senior roster included fifteen girls, Martha had chosen only six juniors that year: Lexie Priessman, Madison Desch, Bailie Key, Katelyn Ohashi, Amelia Hundley, and me. All the other girls had been on the national team the previous year; I was the only newbie in the mix. As the six of us lined up in our red-white-and-blue tracksuits, beaming as photographers snapped our team portrait, all I could think was, *Finally!*

CHAPTER 13

Wheels Up

*"It is not enough to take steps which
may some day lead to a goal; each
step must be itself a goal . . ."*

—Johann Wolfgang von Goethe,
WRITER AND PHILOSOPHER

That could be you, Simone!" one of my teammates at
Bannon's called out. The American gymnasts, famously
nicknamed the Fierce Five, had just won artistic team
gold at the 2012 Olympic Games in London, ahead of the
gymnastics powerhouse nations of Russia, Romania, and
China. It was only the second time in Olympic history
that our country's women gymnasts had finished in first

place; the first had been in 1996 when Kerri Strug of the Magnificent Seven famously executed the final vault with an injured ankle. Now, for the past several days, we'd watched another thrilling victory unfold on a giant screen set up in the gym at Bannon's, where I'd gathered with my teammates and coaches to cheer on Team USA.

We'd all held our breath as Gabrielle Douglas took the all-around gold; as Aly Raisman won first on floor; and as McKayla Maroney came away with silver on vault. Earlier, we'd huddled together to see those three, along with Kyla Ross and Jordyn Wieber, climb onto the podium for the team gold medal ceremony. "The Star Spangled Banner" blared from speakers as the American flag rose on a wire over the magenta-colored arena floor. I had chills. I was imagining what it must feel like to stand on that podium with your teammates, knowing you'd pulled off the big win. The *biggest* win.

That's when one of the girls I trained with called out, "That could be you, Simone!" Her words went through me like an electric current. Immediately, several other girls took up the chant: "2016 Olympics, Simone! You can do it! That will be you!"

I'd just achieved my goal of making the junior national team, and to be honest, I hadn't thought much beyond that yet. I've never liked to look too far down the road. I try to stay focused on the next event, and then the next, to keep from overthinking things and becoming overwhelmed. So I didn't say anything as my teammates excitedly picked me for the next Games, which would be held in Rio four years later.

I just laughed along nervously and rubbed my hands over the goose bumps on my arms. *Wow, I went to training camp with Kyla and Jordyn, and now they're winning Olympic gold,* I thought. *Maybe I can do that myself one day.* In that moment, I quietly asked God to please help me do everything I could to be part of the 2016 Olympics team.

At Nationals Camp the following January, word spread quickly that Kyla Ross and Elizabeth Price would withdraw from the American Cup in March. Both had suffered injuries and needed time to recover. Who would Martha send to replace them?

I'd worked hard at camp that week. I was now more used to the repetitive drills at the ranch, although I was still kind of starstruck by all the big names training next to me. I was starting to develop friendships with some of them, especially with Katelyn Ohashi, a pixie-cute girl who always stood next to me when we lined up for Martha in height order; we were the two shortest girls there.

On the last day of camp, Martha put to rest all the speculation about who would get the upcoming assignment. "The two girls who will be competing at the American Cup this year are"—she paused and looked down the whole line of girls before saying the names—"Katelyn Ohashi and Simone Biles."

Katelyn and I were like, *Yesssss!* We turned to each other and high-fived with both hands; we couldn't have been more excited to be going on assignment together. Martha then announced that Kyla Ross would be the traveling alternate. Even though she wouldn't compete, she'd act as an unofficial mentor for Katelyn and me.

Kyla, Katelyn, and I got really close on that assignment. I loved how smart my teammates were, and how they could always be counted on to perform their routines with consistency, making everything look easy. They both helped me really understand the importance of consistency in my gymnastics, and I learned so much about how to carry myself on the elite competition circuit just from being around them. Katelyn and I had very similar personalities; we were both always giggling about something and liked to have fun. Whenever our coaches saw us together, they'd shake their heads and say, "Oh-oh, here comes double trouble."

Kyla is a lot quieter, but only at first. When you get to know her, you realize she's really funny and a blast to hang out with. She tricks people that way. I remember this one time we were rooming together on an international trip. We had just arrived at the hotel and I went to take a shower, but I couldn't find any full-sized towels in the bathroom. All I saw were a bunch of small hand towels folded on the basin. After my shower, I picked up one of the hand towels and walked out with it wrapped around me.

I said, "Wow, Kyla, this is going to be really tough for you because you're taller than me and the towels here are really small. Look, barely covers my chest."

Kyla cracked up. "Simone, that's a hand towel," she said. She walked into the bathroom, then reached up to a shelf above the shower stall and got me a full-sized towel. "They're up here," she said. "You just couldn't see them, shorty."

"Um, thanks," I said, laughing too.

Kyla made sure I understood that getting the American Cup my first time out was a very huge deal. "Whoa, congrats," she'd told me. "That's a really big meet for your first assignment. Big crowds, lots of publicity and television coverage. But don't worry. Just go out there and have fun."

Easier said than done! I ended up feeling really sick on competition day. My stomach felt as if it was twisted up in knots. I kept stretching and moaning, pain stabbing me with every move. After a while, Martha came over.

"Are you okay?" she asked.

"My stomach hurts a lot," I admitted.

Martha didn't seem that worried, and told me that other gymnasts she'd coached had suffered the same stomach pains when they were anxious before meets.

Once I realized the knots in my stomach were just nerves, the pain eased slightly. I think I was just overwhelmed at having to perform on this big stage in front of Martha. I didn't want her to regret choosing me for the assignment out of all the other girls she could just as easily have chosen. The meet actually went really well until I got to beam. In fact, up until that point, I'd been in the lead, with Katelyn right behind me. But on the beam, I suddenly went crooked on a double back-handspring layout series, and I crashed sideways to the floor.

Oh, I was horrified. On the YouTube video of my beam routine, you can actually see my face crumple as I fight back tears. I remember standing there thinking, *You just fell off the beam on national TV. Your first assignment. You're doomed, Simone.* And the next thought: *What is Martha going to say to you after the meet? Oh my gosh, you're going to be in so much trouble.* At first, that's all I could think about—how mad Martha was going to be, how disappointed. Fortunately, the thought that came on the heels of that one saved me: *Oh, snap! You've got a routine to finish! Get back up on that beam!*

When you fall off an apparatus, you have thirty seconds to remount the equipment. I realized I'd lost track of the time, and so hurriedly, I climbed back up. I finished the routine the best I could, nailing the tumbling part of my dismount but taking a big step on the landing.

"Way to finish!" Aimee said as I came down off the mat. She usually stays really positive during a meet. She figures it does no good to harp on mistakes in a routine that's over and done with when I'm trying to get my head ready for the next event. There's time to correct mistakes later, but at the meet, she'll always find the thing in my routine she can praise. Now, seeing how upset I was, she said, "Calm down, Simone. It's just another meet." But I barely heard her. I was so scared of what would happen when Martha got to me. To make matters worse, television cameras were zooming in on my face, and reporters were following me around, even to the bathroom, waiting to see if I would cry. No way would I let them see me cry.

And you know what? After the meet, Martha wasn't angry at all. In fact, she said she was proud of me! "You've just got to work on that beam routine till you're really confident in it," she said, "but overall, you did really well. Katelyn came first and you came second. It was a good first assignment." She put her hands on my shoulders and rocked me back and forth a little before adding, "Now you just got to get that head screwed on right."

———————

Meanwhile, in my life away from gymnastics, an exciting thing had happened: my parents had agreed to get me a car for my sixteenth birthday. I was super excited to learn how to drive. As soon as I'd turned fifteen, I'd signed up for driver's ed to get my learner's permit. After that, I started bugging my dad to let me get behind the wheel of his truck. He had a better idea. "I think we need to get you a car so that when you take the test, you'll be in a car you're comfortable with," he said. As usual, Dad had done his research. "The Ford Focus is one of the safest cars for teens right now," he told me. "It's top five, so that will be the model you're getting, but I'll let you pick the color." Soon after that, he took me to an auto show, where I picked out a car in this really pretty turquoise blue.

This was right before I traveled to Europe for my first international team camp, followed by meets in Italy and Germany. We'd be gone for the two weeks in March, and I'd turn sixteen while in Italy. Secretly, I hoped that when I got back home, a shiny new turquoise-blue Ford Focus would be waiting for me in our driveway. I was daydreaming so much about that car on my overseas assignment, it helped distract me from the stress of competition—which might be why I performed at those meets as well as I did. At the Jesolo Trophy in Jesolo, Italy, the USA women won team gold, and I won the all-around title, as well as taking first place in vault, beam, and floor exercise. A couple of weeks later, at a meet in Germany, my team again won gold, and I placed first in vault, beam, and floor, taking silver in the all-around behind Kyla Ross.

But when I got home, there was no car in our driveway. I ran into the garage thinking maybe my new car was parked in there, but it wasn't. I thought, *Okay, maybe they're waiting,* and I let it go. I was jet-lagged and too happy about how my meets had gone to dwell on it much. I just shrugged and went to my room, took a shower, and fell right to sleep.

I woke up hours later to find Adria in my room. "Hey, Simone, I got you a birthday present," she said, resting a large package on my bed. I tore open the wrapping paper to find the zebra-print fitted car interior that Adria knew I wanted.

I hugged my sister, and ran into my parents' room to show them what Adria had given me. "Dad, since I don't have a car yet, can I see how it fits the steering wheel and the seat of your truck?" I begged.

"Okay," he said, "but just wait five minutes."

"Wait?" I asked. "Why?"

"Just a few minutes," Mom said, smiling mysteriously. I was totally confused and starting to become a little suspicious. Five minutes later, my parents said, "Okay, let's go to the garage. Let's see how the zebra cover fits the truck."

When I opened the garage door this time, there was my beautiful turquoise-blue car! I started freaking out and jumping up and down and screaming, "I love you, Mom! I love you, Dad!" and hugging them. They told me that our next-door neighbor, Mr. Jim, had hidden the car in his garage, and right when Adria gave me my present he'd been moving the car to our garage.

Later that day, my uncle Barnes came over and helped Dad install the zebra interior in my car. "Are you sure about this print?" Dad said when they were finished. "Your car just looks nuts."

But I loved it. "It's my own special touch," I told him.

Still, I had to admit my father looked really weird against that zebra-print interior. But since I didn't yet have my license, he had no choice but to drive in my car with me. That really motivated him to teach me how to drive, so I could pass my driving test and he wouldn't have to be seen inside my zebra-print car anymore.

My dad taught me the basics in a huge, empty parking lot. Then it was time to take the show on the road. The first time I drove on a highway, with traffic, I was so tense that my legs were like sticks that wouldn't bend. I was actually sore the next day. The whole time, Adria was in the backseat of the car yelling, "We're gonna die! She's gonna kill us all." Thanks, sis!

After a while, I started driving us all the way home from the gym every evening, and my dad went from nervously shouting at me to, "Look left, look right, look over your shoulder, check your blind spot, stop at the stop sign, put on your indicator, watch out for that car," to just sitting quietly beside me as I drove. One night, he actually started snoring.

"Adria, my teacher's sleeping," I said to my sister in the backseat. There was no answer. She was sleeping too.

A couple of months later, I took my driving test. There was a scary moment when rain began to sprinkle and I realized I didn't know how to turn on my windshield wipers. My tester hadn't arrived yet, so I rolled down the window in a panic and called out to my dad, who was waiting on the sidewalk. He leaned in the window and quickly showed me what to do. I ended up getting 100 on my driver's test, even though the tester covered my backup camera with a sheet of paper during parallel parking. You're supposed to do it by looking behind you, but I only knew how to parallel park using that camera! Luckily, the paper slipped off the camera and I stole a quick glance before my tester could notice me doing it. That's how I managed to parallel park perfectly.

When I got home, I quickly discovered why my parents had been so agreeable about me getting my own car. "Well," my dad said, handing me my car's extra set of keys, "you'll be driving Adria to school this year." He explained that as busy as he and my mom were running fourteen nursing homes, in addition to all the drop-offs and pickups at Adria's school and our gymnastics practice sessions, they needed another driver in the family. Plus, in the fall, Adria would be starting ninth grade at a public high school that was half an hour away.

I tried to get out of it. "But, Dad, Adria has to be at school at 6:15 a.m., and I don't have practice till nine. I'm going to have to wake up at, like, five in the morning to get her there on time. That's so not fair!"

"The joys of car ownership," my father said, sauntering away from me cheerfully.

So every morning when I wasn't out of town for a gymnastics meet, I'd roll out of bed and get in the car to take Adria to school. Some mornings my sister would sleep past her alarm or forget to turn it on, and I'd have to bust down her door. "Adria, get up! Get up!" I'd yell. Because if I had to wake up at 5 a.m., she better be up too. Then I'd drive her to school and drive myself back home, thirty minutes each way. That left me with hardly enough time to make breakfast and get myself dressed before driving to morning gym practice forty-five minutes away. It was torture. Thankfully, it only lasted one year because Adria homeschooled with me during tenth grade. But she decided she missed being in public school with her friends and reenrolled there for eleventh grade. By then she had her driver's license and a car of her own, and so I was finally free. But, man, driving her to school was the worst. I still can't believe our parents made me do that!

Just kidding. Everybody knows I'd do anything for my sister.

My sweet new ride wasn't the only perk of turning sixteen. On the competition circuit, I was now considered a senior, going up against Olympic stars like Gabby Douglas, Aly

Raisman, and Kyla Ross. There was no question I could do the big skills, and yet as I went up against these talented girls, a part of me wondered if my recent success was a fluke. *Get that head screwed on right*, Martha had said after my fall off the beam at the American Cup. Her manner had been both stern and kind, as if she believed in my potential.

But as relieved as I'd been that she wasn't angry, I couldn't wrap my mind around the fact that I would've been on track to take first place in the entire meet if I hadn't gone crooked on beam. It's crazy, but instead of that whole experience pushing me to train even harder, I began slacking off in practice. Maybe I was afraid of making an all-out effort and then failing. Worse, what if I kept winning? That was a lot to live up to! Could I really meet such high expectations from everyone? Was I really good enough?

For months, Aimee and I butted heads in the gym, but my casual attitude didn't show in my competitive performance right away. The truth is, I was as astonished as everyone by my rookie success. Unfortunately, no matter how many times Aimee warned, "You need to train as hard as you compete, Simone," I seemed to think I could just get up there during competition and pull a medal-winning performance out of the hat. It was a delusion that would put me on a collision course with reality at the US Secret Classic meet the following July. But that was still in my future. With a streak of wins and a bright new turquoise-blue car in my driveway, I was riding high.

—•—

CHAPTER 14

Saving Graces

"When we least expect it, life sets
us a challenge to test our courage
and willingness to change."

—Paulo Coelho, writer

Chicago, July 27, 2013. By the time I got to floor exercise, I was so tired I could barely feel my legs. I knew what Aimee was going to say—that I hadn't trained seriously enough in the weeks leading up to the US Secret Classic, and my exhaustion now was the result of poor preparation. I'd been mortified at how I'd performed on bars: One second I was flying backward over the high bar in a straddle Tkatchev, the next I was crashing onto my butt, looking up at the bar and wondering how I got there. I never missed the catch on my Tkatchev anymore, and yet today it had happened. The audience gasped as I fell, and I glimpsed Martha Karolyi on the sidelines, her face scrunched in a frown.

I jumped up immediately, remounted the bar, and performed a perfect Tkatchev on my next try. But the damage had been done. The best I could hope for was to turn in clean routines in all my other events. The problem was, instead of shaking off my disaster on bars, I was still feeling sorry for myself as I hopped up onto the balance beam. I was so distracted, I didn't make a single one of my connections, and I wobbled through the routine like a bobblehead toy. At least I didn't fall.

Next up was the floor. I started off well enough. But my lack of conditioning caught up with me on the final tumbling pass. I didn't get enough height to pull off the full rotation in the air, and I came down short, pitching forward onto my knees and almost face-planting into the floor. I jumped right up and finished the event, but I knew I had no chance of medaling now. And that wasn't the worst of it. On that last tumbling pass, I'd crunched my ankles on the landing, and now my right one was aching. But I didn't tell anyone. I was furious at myself. This wasn't how a senior on the national team was supposed to perform.

I started to head over to the vault, since that was immediately after my floor exercise. I was thinking, *Okay, let's just get this over with.* But Aimee noticed me limping, slight as it was, and she took me off to the side.

"I'm pulling you from the meet," Aimee said.

"What? No!" I protested.

But my coach's mind was made up. "Simone, you're not mentally in the game," Aimee said. "And you're in danger of badly injuring yourself. I'm sorry, but I'm not going to let you do that. You're out. That's it."

"Whatever," I said, shrugging like I didn't care. The brat in me popped out in full force.

As I walked away, I overheard another coach commenting to someone behind the stage curtain about my lackluster performance. "You know why you crashed?" he said. "Because she's too fat, that's why. How does she expect to compete like that? Maybe if she didn't look like she'd swallowed a deer, she wouldn't have fallen."

I felt so humiliated by his words that tears came to my eyes. The confusing thing was, I weighed the same as I'd weighed in Italy and Germany when I won gold. So what the coach was saying didn't make any sense to me. Still, I was crushed. In that moment, I felt wrong in just about every way I could possibly feel wrong.

Aimee came to get me then, because Martha wanted to talk to me. When I told her what I had overheard, she was annoyed. "You're not fat," she said as we walked over to meet with Martha. "Just put that out of your head. The problem is how you prepared, or rather how you *didn't* prepare. We'll talk about it later."

If I'd escaped Martha's displeasure before, I was in for it this time. She clucked her tongue and shook her head at me disapprovingly. "Simone," she said, "you're a senior now. This is your year to make a name for yourself, and look at how you went out there. *You* did that to yourself. This is what happens when you're not one hundred percent focused and trained and ready to do what you need to do. So when you go back in the gym these next three-and-a-half weeks before Nationals, I want you to really focus, because if you're having a hard time in practice, you can't expect to just whip out your routines in competition."

I heard what Martha was telling me loud and clear. And I knew what Aimee had said about poor preparation was true too. And so, when I went back into the gym, it was their voices that pushed me to work harder. I wanted to be better and stronger and more consistent for them, and for my teammates, my parents, and myself too. But I couldn't forget what the coach behind the curtain had said about me being fat.

My parents didn't appreciate the other coach's comments about my weight any more than Aimee did, but they encouraged me not to let it bother me too much. Aimee also suggested that it wasn't my weight the coach had been criticizing, but my lines. It was true I was short and muscular, which meant that, unlike long, lean gymnasts, I had to pay extra attention to my extensions and body shape to achieve the most graceful lines. If that was what the coach had been getting at, he sure could have chosen better words. I tried to move on.

In the end, two really good things came out of my terrible performance at the 2013 Secret Classic: I had a one-on-one coaching session with Martha at the ranch, and my parents arranged for me to meet regularly with a sports psychologist.

I'll tell you about the coaching session with Martha first. Actually, I was terrified when I heard that she wanted me to attend a private camp at the ranch. This wasn't typical at all, but since I lived just an hour away from Huntsville, Martha decided that it might be a good idea. She wanted to make sure that I wouldn't fall apart ever again like I'd done at Classics. She knows that once you have a meet like that, you can start to doubt yourself. She'd told Aimee, "We all know this girl has got the power; she just needs to be more disciplined."

So there we were—Martha, Aimee, and me—in the training center at the ranch. First, Martha asked how my ankle was doing. She knew that the week before, I'd seen a doctor who'd treated me to ease the pain and promote healing. "It feels okay," I told Martha now. "It's not hurting at all."

Then, after I'd warmed up with some running and conditioning, Martha asked to me to perform each of my events. Both coaches were completely expressionless as they watched me do my routines—vault, bars, beam, and floor exercise, in the Olympic order—but afterward, Martha came over and held my face in both hands. "Good job, Simone," she said. "Now you just go out and do that at the P&G National Championship in August."

"Thank you, Martha," I said.

But Martha had a lot more she wanted to tell me. She wanted me to understand that my performance at Classics was just "something that happened," and the worst thing I could do was to let it mess with my head. "I know you can do better, Simone, because I've seen you do it," she said. "You went to Italy and Germany with us earlier this year and you did the American Cup, and you did so well at all those competitions. So don't be too hard on yourself. But you do need to own up to your talent a little bit more. Yes, you are very good, and so there will be expectations on you. But that is not for you to worry about, because once you're out there on the floor, it's just you and your gymnastics. Nothing else matters."

I was hugely relieved that Martha was being so understanding. Afterward, Aimee would refer to that meeting at the Karolyi Ranch as my "come-to-Jesus moment," because that's when I really started to turn my bratty behavior around.

My other saving grace in the weeks leading up to the P&G Championship meet on August 17 in Hartford, Connecticut, was my sports psychologist, Robert Andrews. Mr. Andrews is a tall, older man with a direct approach. I'd met with him a couple times before, and had grown to trust him. Now, after messing up in Chicago, I sat in his office and tried to explain how much pressure I'd been feeling.

"Okay, Simone, I hear all that, but let me ask you something else: What do you love to do?"

I didn't even have to think about it.

"I love to have fun," I said.

"And were you having fun at the Secret Classic?"

"No," I responded.

"Why was that?"

"Because I was worrying about what everyone else was thinking about me, and I was trying to live up to everyone's expectations."

He said, "You never did that before, so you don't have to do that now. Don't change what has always worked for you, which is to go out there and just have fun."

That was my breakthrough, the final piece of the puzzle, a moment of clarity that allowed me to go out on the floor three weeks later and relish every moment at the P&G National Championships. And I won! I became the US National All-Around Champion for 2013, taking not only individual gold but also winning silver in all four events. At the end of the meet, I was named to the US national senior team, and a few weeks later, at the qualifying camp in Huntsville, Texas, I was selected for the US World Championship team. I would be representing my country in Belgium that fall alongside Brenna Dowell, McKayla Maroney, and Kyla Ross, with Elizabeth Price as the noncompeting alternate.

I sometimes wonder if any of these amazing things would have happened if I hadn't crashed at the 2013 Secret Classic. My shaky performance in Chicago had shown me that I needed a serious turnaround in my gymnastics, and I was grateful to everyone who'd encouraged me to face my mistakes and focus on the positive. By helping me make peace with the need to work harder and accept responsibility for the talent God had given me, they'd made it possible for me to fall back in love with flying—and to once and for all end my bratty period.

That summer, there was a new girl at Nationals Camp. Her name was Maggie Nichols, and she was from a town called Little Canada, Minnesota. She'd been named to the US senior team that year, but this was my first time at the ranch with her. She was tall and pretty with strong shoulders and well-defined muscles, and she always killed it on her routines. But she hardly ever talked to anyone at camp, and she spent most breaks alone in her room. Seeing her was like looking through a time machine at myself when I was the newbie at camp. I'd been so intimidated by all the sleek, confident girls who'd been going to the Karolyi Ranch together for years that I could barely find my voice. I know that's hard to imagine, since I'm usually super friendly and love to talk and laugh. But it's true: I was once as tongue-tied as Maggie Nichols—until Kyla Ross and Katelyn Ohashi had reached out to me and brought me into the gang.

One day on break, I walked over to Maggie, who was sitting by herself in the cafeteria. "Hey, Maggie, you can come hang out with us in our room when you're done eating," I said.

I saw her face light up and she said, "Okay."

"We'll wait for you," I told her.

But Maggie never showed up. I figured she was as nervous around the rest of the girls as I'd once been, so I went to her cabin and dragged her out of her room. "Come on, Maggie, you're hanging out with us," I insisted. And she did.

Maggie ended up being another saving grace for me that summer. As I helped bring her into the group at Nationals Camp, for the first time I felt as if I truly belonged there myself. I had traveled and competed with all the girls there, and in the pressure-filled environment of training drills and world-class meets, we'd gotten to know each other really well. We'd also shared hilarious moments behind the scenes, trying on each other's makeup, giggling about boys, and coming up with spur-of-the-moment games on long, boring afternoons.

Some people have said the enduring relationships that have grown out of these shared experiences are a part of the secret of Team USA's success: We're all so bonded as a group that in competition, we root hard for one another. We have each other's back. Now, as I looked ahead to my first World Championship in Antwerp, Belgium, on September 30, 2013, it gave me confidence just knowing that when I stepped onto the mat on the other side of the world, I'd have my family in the stands and true friends on the sidelines, cheering me on.

CHAPTER 15

Just Like
Practice

"Stand up and let the world hear your roar;

now spread your wings and begin to soar."

—Mya Waechtler, writer

I wanted to pierce my belly button. On family vacations in Belize, I'd seen girls on the beach with belly rings, and I thought they looked so cool. I imagined myself in crop tops around town, or in a bikini by the pool, my belly ring catching the sunlight.

It all started when I was eight. Mom had given Adria

and me a toy makeup kit with these colorful fake stick-on jewels called bindis. You were supposed to put them on your forehead or at the corners of your eyes, but Adria and I always stuck them on our belly buttons. No surprise, my dad thought this was an outrageous fashion choice. "Why would anyone want a belly piercing?" he asked, genuinely appalled. So I focused all my persuasive powers on my mom. She'd just laugh and say, "Well, I have to think about that."

But one day, just before I turned sixteen, she said, "All right, Simone, if you win Worlds this year, you can get your belly pierced."

This was right at the beginning of my senior season. I hadn't even been assigned to the American Cup yet. At the time, I was only dreaming about being chosen for the Worlds team—maybe as a specialist or even as a noncompeting alternate. It was beyond anyone's wildest imagination to think I could win the biggest international meet of the season, especially my first time, so Mom felt safe shaking on our deal. Dad had no idea we'd made this agreement, and my mom didn't even bother to tell him. She thought it was all a big joke, and she forgot about it almost as soon as we shook hands.

I wasn't thinking about our deal either when I got selected for the Worlds team. Being chosen to compete had been a jaw-dropping moment for me. But now I was riding a wave of excitement and fear. I'd be one of five girls carrying the banner for my country. Could I handle the pressure? I knew this was my test. I'd have to find a way to manage every-one's expectations in order to keep them from making me feel overwhelmed. I needed to learn to how to carry those expectations lightly—like a turtle carries its shell.

This inspiration came to me as I picked out six turtles from my figurine collection to bring with me to Worlds. I'd been taking some of my favorite turtles to gymnastics meets for years, and everywhere I traveled I'd shop for a new turtle figurine to add to my collection. For Worlds, I made sure to pack my lucky turtle, the one with a little red ladybug on its back. The good thing was, I'd be mostly unknown at Worlds. As Martha had told me when she chose me for the team, "Simone, you have nothing to lose and everything to gain at this Worlds. Just take it day by day, and set a name for yourself."

On the first day of competition at the six-day meet, I got an idea. I decided I'd look for Martha on the sidelines before each event, because I knew that if I had her in my line of sight, I wouldn't mess up. Round after round, this strategy seemed to be working for me. I had no clue what our team's scores were, because the other girls and I were just doing our thing, keeping it rolling. After each event, I'd think, *Okay. Cool. Made it. What's next? Let's go.* As we hit one routine after another on that huge stage, our confidence grew. I felt such pride and happiness every time one of my teammates saluted the judges and the audience cheered. To know that I was a part of that was incredible.

I still had moments when my nerves got to me, but whenever I'd start to get anxious, Kyla Ross would remind me, "Simone, just do what you do in practice." And before I went out for each event, she'd high-five me and say, "Just like practice, Simone!" I'd say the same thing to her when it was her turn to go up. "Just like practice" became our catchphrase.

As I walked onto the mat to do my floor exercise, I held on to that phrase like it was a lifeline, because I was about to perform a difficult move I'd come up with in practice—a double flip in the layout position with a half twist out. The way it happened was, I'd landed short on a double layout full out earlier that year during training, and I'd strained my calf muscle on the backward landing. Aimee didn't want me to risk a more severe injury, so she suggested I do the double layout—body straight with legs together and fully extended as I flipped twice in the air—then add a half twist at the end. That extra half twist meant I'd have to master a very tricky blind forward landing, but it would put less stress on my calves.

I thought the new combination sounded incredibly cool, so I started playing around with it until I was landing the skill 95 percent of the time. At the next Nationals Camp, I demonstrated the move for Martha and she thought it looked really good, so we went ahead and added it to the second tumbling pass of my floor routine. I'd already performed the combination at national meets that year, but doing it at Worlds was different. That's because when a completely new skill is executed successfully at a season-ending championship like Worlds or the Olympics, the move will forever after be known by the name of the gymnast who first performed it. Talk about high stakes!

I'll cut to the chase: I nailed the move, which is how it

came to be known as the Biles. How awesome is that! (The only problem is, when I see another gymnast perform the move now, I pray they don't get hurt. I know it's not logical, but because the move is named after me, I'd feel as if it was my fault.)

At the end of the all-around finals, when I saw on the scoreboard that I'd won the gold—that I was the 2013 Artistic Gymnastics World Champion—I couldn't take it in. None of it seemed real. People ask me now, "What was going through your head as you went up to the podium?" and all I can remember thinking is, *Did this just happen?*

Up in the audience, my mom and dad were hugging each other and crying, and I bet they were asking themselves the very same thing!

For the medal ceremony, I lined up with the top eight finishers to march into the arena. One by one, the announcer called us to the stage, starting with number eight and finishing with the top three on the podiums. Kyla Ross had won individual silver (go, Kyla!), and Aliya Mustafina of Russia had won bronze. As the gold medalist, I was the last to go up. Aimee had explained I was to go to each of the top finishers and shake hands to congratulate them before mounting the first-place podium. When I got to Kyla, instead of shaking her hand I hugged her tight, because I really felt as if she was a huge part of my win. From the American Cup onward, she'd been there for me, sharing her experience and just generally showing me what to do.

The medal ceremony was no different. I knew Kyla was used to being on the podium, and I kept watching her so I'd know which hand to take the flowers with, when to hold them up, when to wave, which way to turn for the national anthem, where to go and how to pose for the photographers. During that whole time, I don't think there was anything else going through my head. I was just copying Kyla, following her lead.

And of course, I couldn't really relax yet, because we still had to compete in the apparatus finals over the next two days. In the end, I won four medals at Worlds—two gold for all-around and floor, silver for vault, and bronze for balance beam. Team USA's men and women won twelve medals overall, making 2013 a very good year for our country.

My first morning back in the States, I woke up to a tweet storm. It seemed that the Italian gymnast Carlotta Ferlito had made an unfortunate comment about race to her teammate, Vanessa Ferrari, who had taken sixth in the all-around.

Carlotta's frustration apparently boiled over two days later when I won bronze on beam—ahead of Vanessa at fourth and Carlotta at fifth—and gold on floor, again edging out Vanessa, who took silver. In a video interview that afternoon, Carlotta told a reporter that she'd said to Vanessa, "Next time we should also paint our skin black so then we can win too." I can only guess she was referring to Gabby Douglas becoming the first black woman gymnast to win Olympic gold in the all-around, and to me becoming the first black woman gymnast to win World's just one year later. Whatever she meant, her comment sparked instant pandemonium in the gymnastics community.

But I didn't know about any of this until I woke up and checked my Twitter feed that morning. Everybody was messaging me about Carlotta's comment, asking me what I thought, and being outraged for me. I went to find my mom, who was in her home office, working.

"What in the world are all these people talking about?" I asked her. Together, we googled around and figured out what the whole dustup was about.

"Do not get roped into this," Mom cautioned me as we scrolled through story after story about what Carlotta had said. "Do not let those comments ruin this moment for you, Simone. Just be proud of your performance and the outcome. People will say whatever they want to say, but for you to get into this racism stuff is pointless." She continued: "Of course we know you're black, but that's not the reason you're out there competing. You went to Worlds to represent your country. You're out there simply to do the best you possibly can. So my advice to you is don't even address these comments. If anyone asks you about them, just say you'd rather not respond."

The truth is, I wasn't really bothered by what Carlotta had said. I figured she was just disappointed in the outcome of the meet, and sometimes, when you're not in a good place, you can say the exact wrong thing. So even though the media was in an uproar over her comments, I was totally on the same page as my mom. But what we didn't yet know was that a reporter had already reached my dad on the phone.

The next day, comments he made to the press were quoted everywhere.

"The racial comment was really out of line," he'd said, adding, "Normally it's not in Simone's favor being black, at least not in the world that I live in." The reporter pressed him for a statement on how I was dealing with the controversy. "Simone has moved on," my dad told them. "She's not fazed by it."

I wish I could say that was the end of it, but it would be a few more days before the whole thing blew over. When I went back to training at Bannon's at the end of that week, the girls in the gym were super excited that one of their own had won Worlds. I was in the middle of that happy reunion when a whole series of tweets from Carlotta began coming through. There were about twelve in all.

One said, "I want to apologize to the Americans girls. I didn't want to sound rude or racist. I love Simone and I'm a huge fan of USA gymnastics."

Another one stated "I've made a mistake, I'm not perfect, I was too nervous and I didn't think about what I was saying. I'm just a human. I'm so so sorry."

But even as Carlotta was trying to apologize for the whole affair, a spokesperson for the Italian Gymnastics Federation released a statement on Facebook that just made the situation worse: "Carlotta was referring to a trend in gymnastics at this moment, which is going towards a technique that opens up new chances to athletes of color (well-known for power) while penalizing the more artistic Eastern European style that allowed Russians and Romanians to dominate the sport for years." And he said some other things too, which I won't bother repeating here. Let's just say he was pretty off the mark.

I had easily brushed off what Carlotta said, but the Italian Gymnastics spokesperson's statement *did* bother me a bit. It implied that a power gymnast could not also be artistic and graceful, and also that power and grace were somehow tied to a person's race. I absolutely didn't agree. I'd known celebrated white gymnasts known for their power, like Mary Lou Retton and Shawn Johnson, and black gymnasts praised for their flowing grace, like Dominque Dawes and Gabby Douglas. The point is, all these gymnasts possessed *both* power and grace, and it had nothing to do with their race.

A few days later, the president of the Italian Gymnastic Federation released a new statement apologizing for everything, and people finally moved on. I was glad to put the whole thing behind me, because I wanted every child, regardless of race, to be able to look at my Worlds win and say, *I can dream big too.* I wanted them to know that following your dreams—not just in gymnastics, but in everything—shouldn't have anything to do with the color of your skin. It should only be about finding the discipline and the courage to do the hard work.

My brother Ron told me that when he saw me win Worlds, he dropped to his knees in front of his TV and cried. He was blown away. Speechless. All he could think was, *Oh my God, she did it. My sister is the number one gymnast in the world.* He said he was even a little starstruck when I got home. I thought he was being silly, but I remembered when Ron had called me after I'd failed to make Nationals the first time. I could still hear him saying, "Maybe it's just not your time yet, but your day will come. You're that good, Simone." I'd been so grateful for his belief in me then.

Now he asked me, "How does it feel to win?"

I shrugged, because I still hadn't taken it in.

"I want to go to the Olympics," I said, not really answering his question. "That's my new goal."

Ron threw his head back and laughed. "That's right, Simone!" he said, nodding his head. "You keep dreaming, girl!"

The following weekend, my parents held a big Worlds Party to celebrate my win. There were about four hundred people in our courtyard and backyard and around our pool, and more people were inside the house. Tables were covered with barbecue chicken and ribs, rice and beans, egg rolls, and so many other dishes. We'd hired a caterer to add to the food my mom cooked, and a bartender to set up and serve the drinks. We even booked a DJ for the occasion. As he played music from some of my favorite artists, like Drake and Rihanna, I went around the party greeting everyone.

All afternoon, aunts and uncles, cousins, coworkers of my parents, neighbors, teammates, coaches, and friends wanted my autograph or to pose for selfies with me. I kept a smile on my face, but I was overwhelmed. Meanwhile, all the TVs inside the house were running video of my routines at Worlds, and people would stand around the screens and cheer me on, as if it was happening right then. And everyone had a million questions for me. I loved that they were happy for my win, but it was *a lot* being the center of so much attention.

There would be other parties to celebrate other wins in the years to come, but none would ever feel as intense to me as that first Worlds Party. The only place in the house where I could find a corner of quiet was my bedroom, so at one point during the festivities, I disappeared into my room and locked my door. I just sat on my bed, breathing, listening to the sounds of the party, and refreshing. I checked my Twitter, Instagram, and Snapchat accounts to see what my friends in other places were up to, and I exchanged a few messages with a boy gymnast my age named Alec Yoder, who'd tweeted me, "Congrats on Worlds!" We had several friends in common, and we'd recently started tweeting each other back and forth every day. It had become a friendly contest, to see which one of us would break the daily streak first. I was looking forward to meeting Alec in person at the Houston National Invitational in three months.

After twenty minutes or so of playing around on my phone, I was ready to go back out to the party. But as I started to head back out, I noticed the bag with the turtles I'd taken with me to Worlds sitting in the corner. I'd never unpacked it. I opened it and spread the six turtle figurines on the bed, including the little ladybug turtle that had brought me good luck. Then I decided to unpack the rest of the bag—my sneakers and tracksuits and leos and street clothes. I turned on the radio to listen to music while I put everything away, and right as I did that, the hit song "Burn" by pop artist Ellie Goulding came on.

That song took me right back to the Worlds arena in Antwerp, because it had been blasted over the sound system a hundred times a day during training. And now, coincidentally, it was playing on my radio. I'd heard the song so many times, I knew all the words by heart, so I began to sing along:

We'll be raising our hands, shining up to the sky
'Cause we got the fire, fire, fire . . .

Suddenly, everything I'd just gone through came rushing in: the exhaustion from the Worlds competition, the dream-like medal ceremony, the girls with whom I'd shared the win, my parents looking on in disbelief and joy, my brothers being so happy for me, the photographers, the press, the Italians, Aimee, Martha, all of it. In that moment, the full force of what I had done finally hit me.

I had competed at Worlds. And won.

I really just did that!

As cheerful voices and bursts of laughter from my Worlds Party floated in through my window, mixing with the rhythm of "Burn," I collapsed onto my bedroom floor and started bawling. I was just so proud of myself. And somewhere in there, I also had this thought—*I'm getting a belly ring.*

CHAPTER 16

The Warehouse

*"Change is hard at first, messy in the
middle, and gorgeous at the end."*

—ROBIN SHARMA, WRITER

I marched into St. James the Apostle Church that Sunday in a line of teenagers with solemn faces. It was a few weeks after Worlds, and in a way, our procession reminded me of a medal ceremony, except that no gold, silver, and bronze medals would be given out. Instead, our prize would be something much more powerful: in a few moments, each of us would bow our heads to receive the Holy Sacrament of Confirmation. For Catholics, this moment signifies you have been fully welcomed into the Christian faith community, and that you have pledged to let God's love and grace guide you always.

"Be sealed with the gift of the Holy Spirit," the bishop said as I stood before him with my hands clasped. Using his thumb, he drew the sign of the cross on my forehead with sacred oil and said a prayer for my soul.

"Amen," I whispered when he was done.

"Peace be with you," he said.

"And also with you," I replied before turning and walking back to the pew at the front of the sanctuary, where my confirmation class was seated. As I watched each member of my class take a turn at the altar, I thought about the patron saint I'd chosen as my own the week before, when the bishop interviewed me to assess my spiritual readiness. St. Sebastian had been named the patron saint of athletes and soldiers, because he'd been forced to endure extreme physical trials in his life but was able to heal quickly from his injuries. He's known as the saint who keeps athletes safe and healthy, which is exactly what I needed at the time. I was actually healing from an injury.

In all my confirmation photographs, you can see two little Band-Aids on my right ankle. I'm all dressed up in a little black dress with small lace cutouts at the waist, and wearing heels, and then there are those Band-Aids. I'd recently undergone surgery on that ankle to remove a bone spur. It was a lingering effect from the injury I'd sustained at the Secret Classic in Chicago, when I'd landed short on a rotation and jammed my ankles into the mat, but the ankle still bothered me when I landed just a little bit wrong on a dismount, or when I was tired. On my final floor exercise at Worlds, I'd felt a sharp pain every time I came down from a tumbling sequence. My parents scheduled me for ankle surgery a couple of weeks later.

It was a simple procedure to scope out the calcium buildup, but the doctor explained I'd be put to sleep with anesthesia. He also had me remove my brand-new belly ring; I'd had my belly button pierced just two days before. (Trust me, my mom and I did our research, and we finally chose a place that had a five-star rating and tons of rave reviews.) I was thrilled with my silver belly ring, but now my doctor was telling me that if they had to use a defibrillator to revive me during surgery, the metal in that belly ring could lead to electrocution. So I removed it. No big deal; I'd be wearing it again by the next day. I was way more worried about the operation itself. I'd never undergone any kind of surgery, and to be honest, I was terrified. What if something went wrong and I couldn't do gymnastics anymore?

"Will my parents be with me when I wake up?" I asked the doctor.

"No," he said. "We don't want anyone talking in the room before you wake up. We want you to come out of the anesthesia on your own."

So then I asked the nurse to make sure a blanket my mother had given me one Christmas would go with me into surgery. It had cute little monkeys on the fabric and a fringe of tied-off edges. I was obsessed with that blanket. I just kept saying, "My blanket's got to go in with me, okay? Promise you'll make sure it goes with me into surgery." The nurse promised, and sure enough when I woke up, the blanket was covering me.

"All right, Simone," the doctor said before discharging me later that afternoon, "you'll probably feel some pain and soreness around that ankle, so we're sending you home with pain medicine and an orthopedic boot. You'll be on crutches for about three weeks."

Although I hadn't yet chosen St. Sebastian as my patron saint, he must have been working overtime, because I felt hardly any pain in my ankle after surgery. That's why I ditched the crutches two days later. The Sunday of my confirmation, I begged my mom to let me take off the ortho boot and put on heels. She agreed under one condition: the Band-Aids had to stay. The following week, I forgot about the ankle completely as I raced down the hallway, laughing and chasing Adria in some game we were playing. "Simone, stop running!" Mom shouted from the living room. That's when I remembered I was still recovering from surgery.

Through it all, I only missed two days in the gym, although I only worked on uneven bars and upper body conditioning until the doctor cleared me to do more. Since that time, the ankle has never again troubled me. St. Sebastian—he's my kind of saint.

⸻

Coach Aimee and Coach Tomas didn't seem to be getting along. I didn't know (and still don't know) what their disagreement was about, but they were barely talking. The coldness between them would turn fiery hot just a few weeks later.

One afternoon in February 2014, Adria and I came into the gym and Aimee didn't give us any workout assignments. There were about ten of us team members—mostly level eights, nines, and tens—waiting for instructions. Instead, Aimee said, "You guys can have free time today."

That had *never* happened.

All the other girls started cheering, "Woohoo! Free time! Yeah!"

But something wasn't right.

"You guys, doesn't this seem weird to you?" I said.

"Nah, she's just being awesome!" they insisted.

Adria and I and the rest of the team ran through a few of our routines, and the whole time I was waiting for Aimee to come out and send us to do the stair circuit, because it was stair day. But she never came. Finally, I went with a couple of the other girls to look for her. I found her talking to another one of our coaches in the back.

"Aimee, so what are we doing for conditioning today?" I said.

"I don't care," she said. "Do whatever you want."

One of the girls said, "All right, let's go jump on a chair!" She was joking, of course, but I knew that whatever was going on didn't seem one bit funny.

"Guys, this is weird," I said again.

"Why do you keep saying that?" someone responded. "Just have some fun, Simone. Don't be so serious!"

A few minutes later, everyone could hear Tomas and

Aimee arguing loudly, and then Aimee picked up her bag and left. I can't recall what they were saying; all I remember is being stunned and panicked when I saw Aimee leave.

A few of us went over to Tomas and asked him what was going on.

"Coach Aimee just walked out," he said. He seemed upset and a little dazed. "I think Coach Aimee just quit the gym."

Everyone let out a huge gasp. None of us had seen this coming. By now you know that whenever I feel anything strongly, whether that's fear, sadness, anger, or joy, my default is to cry. I ran to the bathroom because I knew tears were about to overflow, and I didn't want to add to the chaos in the gym. I found my cell phone in my bag and, while sobbing hard, I called my mom.

"Mom, Coach Aimee just left. I don't think she's coming back."

"I heard," Mom said. "She just called me. I'm going to meet her now."

"What should Adria and I do?" I said. "Nobody's coaching us here."

Mom thought for a moment. "There's a faith formation class this afternoon at church," she said finally. "Why don't you and Adria go there right now?"

"Should we clear out our lockers?" I asked. I already knew that if Aimee was leaving, I wanted to go with her. But that made me sad, because it would mean leaving all my friends at Bannon's. It was the only gym Adria and I had ever known.

Mom was levelheaded, as she has always been. "Just leave everything as it is for now," she said. "There's no need to be dramatic here. Just explain to Tomas that I told you girls to go to church. We'll talk about everything tonight."

After letting Tomas know we were leaving, I drove Adria and myself to church for catechism class. Both our eyes were red. When the priest asked me to read something to our group, I suddenly started crying again. As soon as Adria saw me crying, she started to sob too.

"Are you okay?" the priest asked us. He'd never seen Adria and me so upset. As far as he knew, we were two happy-go-lucky girls.

I shook my head. "N-n-not really, but I can't talk about it," I said.

"Why don't you go outside for a bit?" he suggested.

My sister and I spent the rest of the two-hour catechism class sitting in my car in the parking lot. We didn't speak. We just sat there running through scenarios in our minds, trying to figure out what came next.

When we got home, we found out that Mom had spent the afternoon with Aimee at her house, the two of them talking in her living room. Aimee let my mom know she'd decided to leave Bannon's and find another gym, and she was hoping our family would go with her.

Mom didn't even ask Aimee why she left. She didn't want to get in the middle of whatever was going on with her and Tomas. Mom knew Aimee had been at Bannon's for nearly two decades. Aimee had started in 1997, the same year I was born, and she'd gotten married and had her three sons while working there. My mom figured if Aimee had decided to leave now, she must have her reasons. Instead of questioning her about them, my mom addressed the only issue that directly affected our family—whether Adria and I would stay at Bannon's or go with Aimee to her new gym.

"Well, it's not just what Ron and I think," she told Aimee. "It's whether the girls want to go with you. It's really their choice." Then Mom asked her, "So where are you thinking of going?"

"I don't know yet," Aimee admitted. "This is all very sudden, so I don't have a plan. I wanted to discuss it with you first."

Mom jokes now that she must have temporarily lost her mind that day, because the next thing out of her mouth was this:

"Well, why don't I build my own gym?" she said. Aimee stared at her. "That way, Simone and Adria can have a safe and well-equipped place to train and they won't have to gym hop. I really don't want my girls to have to do that."

Mom says the idea just popped into her head out of nowhere, but the more she considered it, the more it began to sound like a good plan. Soon, right there in Aimee's living room, the two began excitedly figuring out just how they'd make it happen.

"How much land would we need?" Mom asked, thinking out loud. "Maybe four acres? Okay"—she snapped open her laptop—"let's see what's available around here." That very afternoon, while Adria and I were moping in the church parking lot, my mom called some brokers and arranged to see a few plots of land for sale nearby. She looked at several pieces of property before the broker showed her a four-acre lot not far from our home.

"It's perfect," Mom said.

My dad had traveled to see a football game in Detroit that week, so Mom called him that Saturday and told him about her crazy plan. "Ron, we're building a gym," she said, and then she gave him the backstory. On Monday when Dad returned, Mom showed him the four-acre plot of land. Two days after that, they actually signed a contract to purchase it.

By this time, Mom had already told Adria and me that Aimee was definitely leaving Bannon's. Mom asked us what we wanted to do. Adria decided she wanted to finish out her level eight season at Bannon's before moving to another gym, but I was sure I wanted to go with Aimee right away. At the same time, I wanted to finish out the week at Bannon's so that I could say good-bye to everyone. I'd learned a lot from all my coaches and teammates there, and I was grateful for all of it.

Still, I knew I wanted to go with Aimee. She'd always helped me keep everything in perspective. For example, unlike some other coaches I'd heard about, Aimee didn't try to control my eating and she wasn't focused on my weight; she just counseled me to eat healthily and to always listen to what my body was telling me it needed. She knew my parents cooked nutritious food at home anyway. Aimee also never made me feel as if the world would stop spinning if I made a mistake in competition. In fact, if I messed up, I was much harder on myself than she ever was. That's because she truly believed the only reason to work hard at gymnastics was for the love of the sport. Even now, when the competition stakes were becoming so much higher, she still encouraged me to train with dedication, then go out there and have fun. That was exactly the balance I needed.

At the time, Mom and her partners in the nursing homes were negotiating to sell the business, which was thriving. My mom and dad agreed that with the money from the sale, they'd be able to build a world-class gymnastics-training center from scratch. The next weekend, when my godparents, Uncle Paul and Aunt Judy, came over to our house, my dad said, "My wife says we're building a gym." Everybody had a good laugh, even my mom. I don't think my parents understood yet the challenge they were taking on.

It's good that my dad was on board with my mom's wild idea, because it took a while for her to find a purchaser for her nursing homes. While she continued to manage that business until it finally sold, my dad was meeting with architects and contractors daily. "I had no idea how complicated this whole process would be," Mom says now. "It wasn't anything like the nursing home business, where we'd look at an existing building and negotiate to buy and then renovate based on what was already there. Building our own gym was way more involved. Suddenly, Ron and I were dealing with city inspectors and county zoning laws; engineers and land surveyors; drainage issues and blueprints and clearing trees and commercial licenses. I cannot tell you how many times I said to my husband, 'If I'd known what we were getting into, we would never have done this.'"

But now they were committed. And if there is one thing everyone knows about my parents, it's that once they put their hearts and minds to something, they never quit.

The World Champions Centre (WCC) in Spring would take more than two years to complete. My parents envisioned it as a family-friendly facility that would offer training in everything from tumbling and taekwondo to dance and cheerleading, ninja warrior, kickboxing, trampoline classes, and competitive gymnastics through the elite level—all in an airy, 52,000-square-foot climate-controlled gym with forty-foot-high ceilings. There would be a giant foam pit, huge helicopter fans, a fitness center for parents, an upstairs viewing area with comfy armchairs, Wi-Fi everywhere, an apparel and accessories store, a café with healthy snacks, physical therapy and rehab rooms, and even a dedicated homeschool classroom with a teacher permanently on staff. And my dad made sure the architects included rows of large windows on every side, allowing sunlight to pour down on us as we practiced.

I didn't take all that natural light for granted because, before we were able to move into our beautiful, spacious, light-filled training center in 2015, Adria and I had been working out in a dingy warehouse over by the railway tracks. But I'm getting ahead of the story.

Right after Aimee left Bannon's, my parents leased space at a gym called AIM, which stands for Athletes in Motion. Adria and I, and four other gymnasts who decided to follow Aimee, trained there for about six months. One of the other coaches from Bannon's, Selinda, also moved with us, so we made up our own little team of eight athletes and two coaches. But it was awkward trying to run our start-up WCC program in the middle of someone else's business. We always had to be aware of not getting in the other team's way, and if we invited people to join our team, instead of AIM's, it got a little weird.

I remember feeling unsettled during that transition, because around that time I'd injured my shoulder and had to sit out the first half of the 2014 competition season. My shoulder had given out on me at Nationals Camp that spring. As one of our exercises at the ranch, we had to hold a handstand for one full minute. I was in the middle of doing that when suddenly my shoulder popped out and I crashed onto my head. Scary stuff. For six months after that, all I did was go to therapy three times a week and do light conditioning that didn't involve the shoulder. I still went to the gym every day, but I didn't touch the uneven bars.

To make matters worse, my parents had thought construction of their World Champions Centre would be farther along by the time our six-month lease with AIM was up in September. They were quickly realizing that building a state-of-the-art facility was going to take a lot longer than they'd imagined. They didn't want to keep subleasing from other gyms, so they began looking for a space where they could set up their own temporary training center.

One day when my mom was driving around, she saw a warehouse across the railroad tracks. She decided to investigate and discovered a car-painting shop on one side of the property and several empty warehouse bays with roll-front gates on the other. She and my dad ended up signing a one-year lease for two warehouse bays that made up a total of 9,000 square feet. They had a hole cut in the wall between the two adjoining warehouses so we could easily get from one side to the other. Then my parents and Aimee began turning the warehouse into a gym, painting all the walls and cleaning the place and bringing in top-of-the-line equipment. They also installed industrial-sized fans, but that did almost nothing to ease the heat and humidity inside the bays. The coaches were afraid we'd perspire and slip on the equipment, so even though we didn't own the warehouse space, my parents paid to install air-conditioning throughout. Safety first.

No matter how much sprucing up we did, that warehouse was *not* pretty. There were always cobwebs high up in the ceiling that we couldn't get to, and the rows of skylights way up above us were grimy and gray, so the gym always seemed dark. Everyone began referring to the space as the Warehouse, even the parents of the kids who trained there. The thing is, even though the building was ugly, we actually had good equipment to train on and great coaches. My mom had hired two more coaches by then, and soon more families began signing up their kids for our programs. When we first moved to the Warehouse, we had eight gymnasts, including Adria and me. By the time the spanking-new WCC building was completed fourteen months later, we had two hundred clients, from preschool tumblers to elite-level athletes.

My parents had been concerned that all the moving around would disrupt my training routine, especially when I had to get back into competitive shape after my shoulder injury healed. It didn't help that Aimee wasn't out on the floor coaching as much as she used to be. During the six months I'd been taking care of my shoulder, she'd been running the entire gymnastics program at the Warehouse—including all the compulsory and optional JO levels. That often kept her holed up in the office taking care of a mountain of paperwork.

When I finally returned to training full time, Aimee trusted the other coaches, Terry and Tamara, to give me what I needed when she wasn't there, and for the most part, they did. But what she didn't realize was that I'd left Bannon's because it was *her* coaching style that made the difference for me. I'd grown up with Aimee. I'd traveled the world with her. She felt like a dependable big sister who didn't take any mess and always gave it to me straight. I missed her.

One day, when I was being a little sulky during practice, Aimee came over to me. "What's going on?" she asked me, and to her surprise, I broke down. "You're never out here!" I burst out. "You never coach me anymore! You're just always in the office! You don't even care!"

Aimee look startled, and then her face crumpled. I was instantly sorry about what I'd said. "Oh, Simone, I'm so sorry," she said, hugging me. "I'm right here. I haven't gone anywhere. I'm always right here."

Even now, when Aimee talks about that day, her voice quivers. After that, she got someone else to take over most of the office paperwork (it wasn't what she wanted to be doing anyway), and she began actively coaching me again.

Just three months later, in August 2014, Aimee was with

me when I won the all-around title at the P&G National Championships in Pittsburgh, Pennsylvania, becoming the US Champion for the second year in a row. I also took gold on vault and floor and tied for silver on beam with Alyssa Baumann. Afterward, I was once again chosen for the national team and selected to compete on behalf of my country at the World Championships, which would be held in Nanning, China, in October. My second time at Worlds would be a way more stressful one. Let me explain.

After every Olympics, a lot of gymnasts take time off, and others retire completely, which means that some countries can't field a full team the following year. That's why the first World Championships after an Olympic year is always an individual meet with no team competition. At my second Worlds, the setup would be different because this was both a team and an individual competition. We all understood that the team medal was the most important one, which meant that if I made a mistake, I wouldn't only be jeopardizing my own chances, I'd also be letting down my teammates and maybe even putting a team win at risk.

It turns out I was worried for no reason. In October, Team USA took top honors in the women's artistic competition, and I won my second all-around World Championship title. I also earned gold on beam and floor and silver on vault. I didn't make the event final for bars, because I'd downgraded the difficulty of my routine; I'd taken out one of my Tkatchevs so I could go easy on my shoulder. But I was happy with how bars had gone anyway: Even though my D score (degree of difficulty) was low, my E score (execution) had been the highest one on my team. Coming back from a shoulder injury, I'd managed to turn in a polished performance on bars, my nemesis. I'd take it.

Later that evening, as I waited with the other winners to be called to the podium for the medal ceremony, I thought about all the upheaval and change I'd just been through. I'd begun the year by leaving the only gym I'd ever known. I'd sat out the first half of the competition season with a shoulder injury, and when I was finally healed from that (good old St. Sebastian!), I'd had to train in an old, dark, cobwebby warehouse. "This has truly been a walk of faith," my mom had said to me just before I left for Nanning. And she was right. What a difference a year makes, especially when you can count on loved ones to lift you up and God to pull you through.

Right then, an announcer called the winners to the floor. Feeling grateful and happy to be among them for a second year in a row, I climbed onto the first-place podium to accept my medal and the ceremonial bouquet of flowers. As the music of "The Star Spangled Banner" filled the arena, I had no idea that what happened next would become a hilarious part of my Worlds story.

——•——

CHAPTER 17

Staying Grounded

"No great thing is suddenly created."

—Epictetus, philosopher

I t became known as "the bee incident"—my battle of the buzz that went viral in a matter of hours. In practically every account of the 2014 World Championship in Nanning, there was some mention of the bee that climbed out of my bouquet of flowers as I stood on the gold medal podium.

During that ceremony, silver medalist Larisa Iordache of Romania stood on one side of me, and Kyla Ross, who'd won bronze, was on the other. Larisa saw the bee first. When the three of us turned to face our country's flags as the American national anthem played, I'd placed one hand over my heart and held my bouquet behind me with the other hand. All through "The Star Spangled Banner," Larisa watched the bee crawling over my flowers. When the music stopped and we faced forward again, Larisa leaned over to me and pointed.

What is she pointing at?

"Simone," she said, "look, there's a bee."

I saw the tiny thing just as it lifted its wings and tried to land on my hand. Suddenly frantic, I held the flowers as far away from me as I could and began shaking the bouquet, hoping to dislodge the bee. I fought against my instinct to toss the flowers onto the floor. I knew no one but Larisa, Kyla, and me could see the insect, and I didn't want anyone to think I was being disrespectful.

Then the bee launched itself right at my head! I jumped down off the podium and tried to dodge and duck, but the buzzing thing just kept following me. I ran one way and then the other, but the bee was still with me. When it dived back into my flowers, I finally threw the bouquet on the ground, hoping I wasn't insulting our host nation. By this time Kyla and Larisa were giggling nervously, and I can only imagine what the audience must have thought at the sight of me running in circles behind the podium.

A moment later, the bee flew out of my flowers again, and I carefully retrieved the bouquet. But now the silly thing landed on Kyla's flowers. With great composure—much more than I'd shown—Kyla laid her bouquet delicately at the edge of her podium and climbed onto my podium with me. Larisa jumped up onto the podium to join us, and the three of us, realizing just how crazy the episode must have looked, burst out in laughter. The whole time photographers were snapping away, and TV cameras were pointed at us, so we finally got it together and straightened up to pose for the winners' picture. In the photograph, Kyla is not holding a bouquet.

The video of the bee incident was everywhere the next day. My mom called my brother Ron from China to complain that I'd ruined my special moment with what she called "typical Simone antics." She said she and my dad had been feeling so proud and emotional, watching from the audience as I received my second World Championship all-around gold, and then suddenly I was jumping down from the podium and hopping around like a maniac.

Ron, who'd watched the bee chase on TV and laughed till his sides hurt, helped Mom feel better about the whole thing. "That's Simone for you," he told her. "She's just always been a goofy and down-to-earth kid. And you know what, it might actually be good for people to see who she is. What you see is what you get with Simone."

I loved that Ron said that about me, because I really did try to be myself. And that included not taking myself and even my gymnastics too seriously. When I'd fallen into that trap before, at the US Secret Classic in 2013, the results had been disastrous. Now I knew to take each day as it came and to do my best. I tried to stay conscious of how incredible it was to be traveling the world with some of my best friends, having adventures together, and knowing that on any given day any one of us might come up with the win.

Martha Karolyi wasn't always such a big fan of me being Simone, though. I remember when I did my first few assignments as a brand-new national team member, I'd congratulate the other girls after their routines. I was just being friendly. As I got to know some of the international competitors better, I'd hug them when they came down from the mat or high-five them and say something like, "You did great!" or "Awesome job!"

Martha took me aside. "Simone, what are you doing?" she said. "You can't go around talking to everybody and cheering and waving like that. It's not how we operate. You have to stay serious and focused here. Just concentrate on your own routine."

I realized that Martha thought me being so social with the other girls meant that I wasn't staying mentally in my zone. But over time she began to understand that what she saw as a distraction was actually good for me. If I focused too hard on my upcoming routine, I'd start to get all nervous and tense. It was better for me to think of competition as an extension of what I did in practice every day. I had to trust that my body knew what to do.

As Ron would remind me in the pep talks he sometimes gave me before meets, "Simone, you do this for six hours every day, six days a week. You've got this. Don't let nerves get to you. Think of it as just another day, another competition, and go out there and enjoy yourself. You've walked your journey, and this is your moment. Embrace it. Just leave it all out there on the floor, and see what happens."

What happened was that Martha eventually decided that since I was winning, she'd just let me be myself. She stopped trying to contain my natural friendliness, and over time the rest of the team relaxed a bit more as well. That's because Martha no longer insisted that everyone be so stern-faced on the sidelines. She made her peace with the slightly looser vibe among all the girls on the team, because she saw that it wasn't hurting us.

That didn't mean Martha went any easier on us in training.

Not one bit.

———

In September 2015, I traveled with the seven-member US women's team to compete at Worlds for my third year in a row. The meet was in Glasgow, Scotland, this time, and we got there a week early to allow our bodies to adjust to the time difference. The last thing Martha needed was a bunch of bleary-eyed, jet-lagged girls on a four-inch-wide beam.

All year, people had been tweeting me, *Three-peat, three-peat, three-peat.* Everyone was telling me I could make history by winning Worlds a third consecutive time. Not only would I be the first American woman to do that, but if I delivered strong performances in the event finals, I could also become the most decorated American gymnast in Worlds history. As astonishing as that was for me to think about, since winning Nationals in 2013 I hadn't lost a single meet in which I'd competed in all four events. I was the three-time US national champion and the two-time World Champion, which meant people's expectations of me in Glasgow were sky high.

I was used to that sort of pressure by now. Or at least I thought I was. My usual way of dealing with it was to put it out of my mind and focus on getting good workouts. But in Glasgow, leading up to the meet, our training days were so rigorous and long that I began to feel exhausted. Maggie Nichols and I were rooming together, and she admitted to feeling worn out as well. We weren't the only ones. All the girls seemed fatigued, but no one dared to complain. That would have made us appear weak and unprepared, and might even get us pulled from the rotation.

I remember I'd brought a banana back to our room to eat after the first day of practice. But I didn't eat it that day, or the second day. Day after day, I kept saying, "Oh, I'll eat it tomorrow." And then I didn't eat it because the skin had started to get brown and the fruit was mushy inside. That poor banana just stayed there, deteriorating. Maggie and I made a big joke of it: Every day we'd pick up the wilted thing. "Oh my gosh, this is us," we'd say, cracking up. "Our energy is just draining away."

A few days later, Maggie's coach brought a new bunch of bananas, and somewhere there is a phone video of Maggie yelling, "Simone, we've got bananas!" and the two of us dying laughing. You know when you've had a really long day and you're so punchy with tiredness that everything seems hilarious? That was Maggie and me.

We did get to rest up a bit before the meet, but by then I'd started to obsess over my routines in a way that's never good for me. I was dreaming about every move at night, and when awake, all I could think was, *I've done fifty routines in practice and I haven't fallen on one. What if I go up there and miss the one?* No matter how I tried to talk myself out of those thoughts, I couldn't seem to shut down my brain.

By the time I got out onto the floor, there was so much extra adrenaline pumping through me that I overpowered a couple of my skills. I was able to regain control, except on one of my tumbling passes on floor, I went too hard into the somersaults and landed out of bounds. But the worst moment came in my beam routine, when I let myself get distracted by the crowd.

Being in Scotland, I knew the audience was going to cheer extra loud for the gymnast from Great Britain, who was finishing up on floor right as I mounted the beam. In competition, there will always be routines happening simultaneously, and the crowd is always going to go nuts for the home team. I'd learned how to brace for that. But that day I didn't time it right. The crowd cheered earlier than I expected, throwing off my concentration. I was right in the middle of a front tuck, and I started toppling. But I grabbed the beam with both hands and held on for dear life. I was thinking, *I don't care how hard you have to grab this beam, Simone, just don't fall.* A fall would have been a much bigger deduction than touching the beam, so I was determined to stay on. And I did.

Despite my slight missteps on beam and floor, I was in first place on both and third on vault. I knew it was because my start values across the board had been high, and my D scores (difficulty) had helped push me over the top. My E scores (execution) were decent too. I guess we'd done so many pressure sets in training all week that at some point my body went on autopilot. That's what saved me. At the end of the meet, the scoreboard showed that our team had once again taken gold—and I'd won the all-around for the third time. My teammate Gabby Douglas earned the silver, and Larisa Iordache of Romania, who'd shared in my ridiculous bee adventure the year before, won bronze.

Still, unlike the excitement I'd felt the first two times I won Worlds, this time all I wanted was to go back to the hotel and climb into bed. It was late in the evening, and I just felt numb. I wasn't even sure I'd read the scoreboard correctly.

"Aimee, I did it, right? I won?"

"You sure did," she said, hugging me.

Before the meet, some reporters had shared that they'd already written the story of me winning, and that if I lost, they'd have to pull the piece and craft a new story. "So you better win this, Simone!" they'd told me, laughing. I'd laughed along, but it had felt like an unbelievable amount of pressure. So when Aimee confirmed I'd won, I exhaled. I was relieved that I hadn't disappointed the people who'd been rooting for me, but in an odd way, this win felt like it belonged more to them than it did to me. "Well, you got your three-peat," I whispered as I left the arena.

On my way back to Texas, I suddenly remembered that during my two weeks in Scotland, the World Champions Centre had opened for business. My parents had been busy moving all the equipment and mats from the Warehouse to WCC while I was competing at Worlds. I could hardly wait to see that wide-open, airy space when I got back to Spring. I was grateful that I'd be walking through those doors for the first time as a three-time World Champion. I'd had a couple of wobbly moments, but in the end, I'd lived up to WCC's name.

A week later, I was at the mall with Adria and people kept watching me. I thought maybe I was imagining it, but some people actually nodded in my direction and smiled. Others looked away quickly when I met their eyes, as if embarrassed to be caught staring. I glanced down to make sure I hadn't buttoned my yellow silk shirt wrong or something, but no, my clothes were fine.

"Why are these people looking at me?" I whispered to Adria.

We'd stopped for smoothies at a Jamba Juice pop-up booth in the mall, and had found a seat at one of the nearby tables. Now, as I sipped my Orange Fusion concoction, I felt several sets of eyes studying me.

"Adria, do I know any of these people?"

"No, but maybe they know you," Adria said, indifferently slurping her Strawberry Whirl.

"Don't be silly, Adria. Why would they know who I am?"

As I said those words, a tiny girl with her blond hair in a ballerina topknot walked over to our table. She looked like she was about eight. An older woman, probably her mother, stood a few steps behind her, smiling at us.

"Are you Simone Biles?" the girl asked me shyly.

"Yes," I said.

"Would you mind if I took a picture with you?"

"Sure," I agreed, even though I was a little puzzled by her request.

The girl put her face next to mine, and her mom snapped a photo with her phone. The girl thanked me and walked away, beaming.

"That was bizarre," I said to Adria, watching them leave. "Why do they know my name?"

Adria rolled her eyes and looked at me as if I was the craziest person on the planet. "Duh," she said. "Wake up, Simone. You're only the three-time gymnastics world champion."

I stared at Adria, realizing just how big a deal my win at Worlds had been. For a fleeting moment, I wished I could see the hugeness of that achievement from the perspective of other people. Don't get me wrong, I'd worked hard to get where I was, and I was thrilled to have won gold, but inside I was still just Simone sitting next to her bored and unimpressed sister in a Houston mall.

"Don't get a big head or anything," Adria said, angling her straw to get the last sip of her smoothie. "I mean, you might be World Champion and everything, but so what?" As soon as she said that, Adria whacked me on the arm to let me know she was kidding, and we both burst out laughing.

"Okay," she said. "I'll admit it. My sister's pretty cool."

CHAPTER 18

Bora-Bora

*"The size of your dreams must always
exceed your current capacity to achieve
them. If your dreams do not scare
you, they are not big enough."*

—ELLEN JOHNSON SIRLEAF IN *THIS CHILD WILL BE GREAT*

Carly, our UCLA team host, dumped a pile of red, purple, orange, and blue scarves on her dorm room bed then laid out a set of olive green T-shirts with Teenage Mutant Ninja Turtle images on the front. But she wasn't finished. She reached into another bag and brought out a tangle of wildly colored tutus, several pairs of black tights, and some turtle-green socks.

"We're all going to the basketball game tonight as Ninja Turtles!" she announced to the seven of us girls on a two-day recruiting visit, which happened to fall on Halloween. "Okay, everyone, choose your colors!"

Colleges with strong NCAA Division 1 gymnastics programs had been scouting me since I was thirteen years old. Over the years, coaches had come to see me practice at Bannon's and later at WCC. I'd also been invited to visit several schools and was excited at the prospect of eventually competing for a top-ranked team. Next to going to the 2016 Summer Games in Rio, doing college gymnastics was my most heartfelt dream.

The University of Alabama had emerged as my parents' early favorite. They were impressed with the facilities there, and the school's winning record, but I felt more at home at UCLA. Some of the girls I knew from Nationals Camp were already enrolled there, and I'd had an instant connection with Valorie Kondos Field, aka Miss Val, their coach. She'd visited me in Spring the year before to assess my skills and recruit me for her Bruins team. She was a lot like Aimee: she believed gymnastics should be fun and that the team should be a family. Miss Val thought I'd be a good fit for her squad, and I thought she'd be a good fit for me.

That feeling had only grown stronger during my campus visit. By the second afternoon, I'd pretty much decided that after I graduated high school in June 2015, I wanted to be a Bruin. The more time I spent in the company of Miss Val's team, the more I wanted to finish out my gymnastics career as part of UCLA's program. And I wasn't the only elite-level girl who dreamed of attending the school. In fact, two of my friends on the national team, Kyla Ross and Madison Kocian, were with me on that overnight visit. The first day, we'd watched the gymnastics team perform in an intramural exhibition meet, and then we'd attended a football game. That evening, I'd be cheering on the Bruins' basketball team with my tutu-wearing Ninja Turtle crew.

I chose a purple color scheme, of course—it was still my favorite color. Kyla chose red. We folded the scarves into headbands and wrapped them around our heads.

"Tied at the front or at the back?" Kyla asked me, spinning the knot of her scarf to the crown of her head and fanning her long black hair over her shoulders.

"Front," I said. "It looks kind of cool with your hair like that."

I wore my own headband across my forehead and tied over my hair at the back with the ends hanging down, like my purple Ninja Turtle namesake Donatello. All the girls huddled together, taking selfies with our phones and making crazy faces to send to our friends on Snapchat. In the midst of the happy, talkative commotion, I remember thinking, *This is so my scene.* I'd been imagining times like this ever since making the decision to be homeschooled. I'd missed out on all the social experiences of high school, and even though Adria kept joking that I could be her date for prom, it would never be the same as attending my own. With college, I'd have another chance at all that. I'd finally get to have the homecoming games and school dances, study groups and student clubs, and all the crazy spontaneous times with friends. That night, for example, we all went for ice cream after the game, and then, since it was pouring rain outside, we holed up in the dorm, chatting with our hosts and soaking up stories of college life.

When I got back to Spring, I wanted to call Coach Val right away and commit to UCLA for the following fall. My parents urged me to wait. They wanted me to consider the University of Alabama, because it was closer to home and didn't have all the distractions of a big city like Los Angeles. But I kept pressing.

"I really want to commit to UCLA," I said.

Finally, my mom said, "You know what, Simone, do what you want."

She said it like she didn't really agree with me, but I'd worn her down. And I ran with it. The next day, while I was alone at home, I dialed the number on the card Coach Val had given me.

"Hello, Miss Val, this is Simone Biles, and I just want to let you know I'm committing to UCLA for college, but if I make the Olympic team, I'll need to defer enrollment for a year."

Miss Val was so ecstatic at my news that she screamed. I felt as if my future in gymnastics was now set, and I couldn't wait to be a Bruin. If only I'd known it wasn't going to be so easy.

———— ⊞ ————

I'd been at this fork in the road before. The last time, when I'd had to choose between high school with my friends or homeschool, was after my devastating failure to make the 2011 national team. Now I was at a similar crossroads, one that might require me to give up my dream of a traditional college experience with my peers. This time, my dilemma was the result not of failure, but of success—my back-to-back all-around wins at the 2013 and 2014 Worlds, which had brought sponsors to my door.

So once again I had a choice to make: Should I work toward my dream of one day competing in the Olympics? Or should I hold onto my goal of pursuing an NCAA gymnastics career and having the "normal" college life I'd fantasized about for so long? If I wanted to go to the Olympics, it made sense to turn professional, which would make me NCAA ineligible. On the other hand, going pro would bring me the kind of financial security that amateur gymnastics could never give me.

I played with the idea of turning pro when I was done with college, but I knew the timing wouldn't work. Sponsors wanted me now, in the run up to the 2016 Olympics in Rio. Turning pro in advance of Rio was the sure thing. I'd be twenty-three when the Olympics came back around in 2020. There was no way to know if I'd still be at the top of my game. Gymnastics wasn't like soccer or swimming or track and field, where athletes could qualify multiple times. Most female gymnasts only go to the Olympics once.

For many athletes, the decision about whether to turn pro might have seemed like an easy one. Money talks. But can I explain the deep sense of loss I felt at the thought of giving up college gymnastics? For years, I'd imagined the camaraderie of team practice, the adrenaline rush of competition, and maybe even being noticed on campus as one of the school's athletic stars. These were the experiences that my gymnastics friends who were already in college were always telling me about on Snapchat and Instagram. They were following the exact same path I dreamed of taking—and they were having fun.

Here's what I found difficult to accept: I had to choose between college and turning pro while talented male gymnasts got to turn pro at the end of college. Their skill level tended to peak at around age twenty-two, when they were older and stronger, which meant they were able to enjoy competing over a much longer period. But for girls, the more our bodies matured physically, the less easily we soared and flipped and twirled through the air. Our gymnastics life span was shorter. Most of us peaked in high school. It just didn't seem fair.

It was true that American gymnastics had evolved in recent years, with older girls like 2012 Fierce Fivers Aly Raisman and Gabby Douglas now back in contention to make the 2016 Olympics team. But the juniors coming up behind us were so good that it was just a matter of time before they pushed us out. With college, at least I'd be guaranteed four more years as a student athlete.

Everyone had an opinion about the choice I was facing, but, of course, no one could make the decision for me. As my friend, the 1996 Olympic gymnast Dominique Moceanu, told me, "This is your future, Simone. You make up your own mind." My mom echoed the same sentiment. "We can tell you what we think," she reminded me, "but not what to do."

And what did my family think?

Mom: "You can always go to college, Simone, but you won't always be able to turn professional. That's a once-in-a-lifetime opportunity."

Adam: "If you have the talent to go pro and don't do it, that would be pretty stupid. You might always regret it."

Dad: "Every Olympic year, there are only a few select kids in the world who have a chance to go professional in something they love doing. You are one of those kids, Simone. Whatever you decide, the main thing is to respect your talent."

Ron had the most to say. He'd called me from a gas station in Louisiana, where he'd traveled on business. "Simone, if I were in your shoes and had the chance to be well compensated for something I enjoy, I'd go for it. I mean, you're doing a full-time job already, so why not get paid for all the hours you put in? Real talk: Are you going to the Olympics? Yes, probably. And then you're going to go back to college? Really? Look, I've been to college, and while it's great, it can't compare to what you're doing. Look at all the places you've been; all the challenges you've overcome. And now you have these great sponsors knocking on your door. And let's be clear, Simone—this is your deal. Mom, Dad, Adam, Adria, me, we don't need anything from you. We're all blessed, and we are set up. So this is not about you taking care of us. This is your chance to set yourself up—your future family, your future children. To be honest, Simone, if I were you, I'd do it."

Compared to Ron, Adria was brief and to the point: "Whatever, Simone. Do what you want. Just stop asking me what I think!"

After weeks of agonizing and praying for guidance and weighing my family's loving advice (yes, even Adria's), this is how I finally explained the decision to myself: *Okay, Simone, you're giving up one of your dreams for an even bigger dream that you're chasing—Olympic success, and everything that comes with it, including your face on the cereal box and maybe even your own line of leos. You're giving up a smaller dream for a bigger one that you actually have a chance of achieving. You can still go to college afterward.*

So in July 2015, I made the decision to turn pro—which meant I now had to make one of the hardest phone calls of my life.

For almost a week, I'd been putting off the call to let Coach Val know I wouldn't be enrolling at UCLA after all. Maybe it was because telling Miss Val about turning pro meant I was truly closing the door on being a Bruin. She'd been so excited when I'd committed, and I hated to disappoint her now.

I tried to get my mom to make the call for me, but she just looked at me like I was crazy. "You made the call to commit to UCLA all by yourself," she said. "I'm quite sure you can make this call too."

Finally, I mustered up the courage and called Coach Val's number.

"Hello, Miss Val, this is Simone." My voice was quavering. "I'm calling to say I'm going pro, so I won't be able to compete for UCLA next year."

Long pause.

"Oh, Simone," she finally said. "I knew the minute I saw your name on my phone what you were going to say."

"I'm sorry," I mumbled, feeling miserable.

"Oh, no, no, don't be sorry," Coach Val said. "I always knew there was a chance I might lose you. But I'm really happy for you. I want you to know that I support you no matter what. Besides, you'll always be my Bruin, because technically, you committed to coming here before you turned pro."

Then Coach Val told me that I was still welcome to come to UCLA when my professional gymnastics career was over. I was relieved to think that even if I couldn't compete, I could still one day be a Bruin. I thanked Coach Val for all her encouragement, and we ended the call. After a few minutes, I tapped the Twitter icon on the phone and tweeted out to the public that I was officially turning pro.

Right away, Coach Val tweeted back a reply: "Enjoy the journey and best wishes for a bright future, Simone." That's when I cried.

A few days later—after I'd moved past my tears—I actually began feeling excited to find the right agent, someone I'd feel comfortable with, who could share in my dream. I consulted with my mom and dad. We threw a couple names around, discussed pros and cons, and our personal opinions started to emerge. After some more research, we all finally agreed on one person, and I made that call.

The process of choosing an agent was a strange new experience for me. I'd spent so many years intensely focused on gymnastics that it felt odd to talk to people about their perspectives on my life outside of the gym. As those conversations took place, the one thing that stood out for my parents and me was the personal connection I felt with the agent I ultimately chose, Janey Miller from Octagon. Rather than encouraging me to brand myself to appeal to sponsors, her goal was to select prospective sponsorships that would be personally meaningful to me. To get an idea of the brands that might be a good fit, Janey asked me to make a list of everything I liked to eat and drink, what particular leos and outfits made me feel pretty, and what products I liked to use in my everyday life. We all appreciated her approach, and I felt good signing with her. My life as a professional athlete had officially begun.

———

My mom and I had just finished up a morning meeting with my financial adviser. Mom had gone to walk the woman to her car while I went to the WCC kitchen to heat up a slice of pizza for lunch. I was leaning against the counter, waiting for the microwave to beep, when my brother Adam, the gym's general manager, walked in.

"Did she leave?" I asked him.

"She just drove away," he said. "How did it go?"

"Good," I told him, "but so weird."

"Why weird?" Adam asked, frowning.

"Who has a financial adviser at my age!" I exclaimed. "It's just weird!"

Guided by my parents and my new agent, Janey, I'd

recently signed endorsement deals with several companies that sold products I loved and could relate to. Now, my parents wanted to make sure I had help managing what was coming to me. I appreciated their business savvy and the way they always looked out for me, but the last thing I wanted to think about on the eve of my nineteenth birthday was financial planning.

"Well, what did she say?" Adam asked me now.

"She wanted me to tell her something that I've always wanted," I said. "She told me to think of something really big."

"What did you say?" Adam prompted.

"I didn't have a clue!" I said, exasperated. "I barely know anything about the world outside of gymnastics!"

"There has to be something you want to do," my brother insisted. "Some part of the world you've always wanted to see, maybe?"

"I told her I want to take a five-day vacation in Bora-Bora with a couple of my friends," I admitted. "I've seen pictures, and it's so beautiful there. It's like this magical place you don't think you'd ever be able to go to except it exists right here on earth with us. But I bet it's expensive. What do you think? Could I even afford that?"

Adam laughed so hard when I said that, tears were streaming down his face. "Oh, Simone," he said. "That's it? That's the big thing you came up with? I kind of think you'll be able to manage a vacation to Bora-Bora anytime you want. I'm pretty sure you've already made enough to do that."

"Well, alright then!" I said, pumping my fists in the air as the microwave beeped. "Bora-Bora, here I come!"

As you can probably tell, I'd spent so many years inside my protected gymnastics bubble, I was only just beginning to understand the benefits of turning pro. But there was also a price to pay. That's because once I turned pro, gymnastics became my job. I'd officially started my career. Suddenly television crews might follow me around in the gym, and reporters would want to interview me for stories, and I'd need to express my personality and be gracious and hopefully sound intelligent. And maybe an endorsement contract might require me to show up at a certain number of sponsored events or to tape a certain number of TV commercials to air during the Olympics and afterward.

These responsibilities were nothing new for me. Even before I turned pro, the media frequently interviewed me and so I was used to performing in front of cameras. The difference was that I now had an agent who could help me manage my schedule. That was a good thing, because the extra responsibilities could sometimes take away from practice time. I knew I had to continue to train hard and do well at meets, because I'd been chosen to be the face of major brands, and I wanted to make them proud. At the same time, I had to keep everything in perspective, because in a few years my gymnastics life would be over and the rest of my life would begin. I wanted to be able to look back and say I had a good run and made some great memories along the way.

As I sat eating my pizza, I tried to remember that I always performed better if I was just plain having fun. That mindset seemed to work best for me. In three consecutive trips to Worlds, I'd earned fourteen medals, ten of them gold, which made me the most decorated American female gymnast ever. I'd also earned more Worlds medals than any other woman in the history of the sport, which put me in the record books—and made me a favorite to make the USA Olympics team. Now, in the months leading up to Rio, I remained determined to enjoy every minute. That meant not thinking too far beyond my next meet, yet preparing every minute for the big event.

At the Pacific Rim Championships in April 2016, I debuted a brand-new, upgraded floor routine set to fast, upbeat samba music that I thought would go over well with the crowd in Rio. I also rolled out a ridiculously difficult second vault, called the Cheng, to go with my Amanar. I managed to nail the execution of both and got the coveted thumbs-up from Martha. Pac Rim had been my first outing of the season, because Martha was picking and choosing all of our assignments carefully. She wanted to minimize the risk of injury before Rio and also make sure her Olympic hopefuls wouldn't burn out before the Games. Her theory was that our performances needed to be at ninety percent by the P&G National Championships in St. Louis in June, and at full throttle two weeks later at the Olympic trials in San Jose, California. The goal was for us to then stay at one hundred percent through the Olympics.

It's a good thing Martha had us aim for ninety percent at Nationals, because we seniors definitely weren't operating at one hundred percent. In the final rounds, some of us went crooked on bars or wobbled on beam or took little hops on our dismounts. There were even a couple of heart-stopping falls. It was late on Sunday night by then, and we'd been continuously training for days. I actually didn't mind that our missteps were so visible. People needed to know that even the best, most accomplished gymnasts get tired.

Though some reporters had referred to me as "the robot" because of my consistency in competition, I was as human as the next girl. Let me tell you, I have as many bad practices and hard days as every other person on the team. The bottom line: There's no such thing as perfection in gymnastics. You do your best, but anything can happen—which is why you have to learn to forgive yourself and quickly move on.

The final night, even with my own bobble on beam and a not-quite-vertical handstand on bars, I came away with my fourth-straight National Championship win. Olympic veteran Aly Raisman turned in a beautiful performance to win silver, while Laurie Hernandez, a bubbly newcomer to the senior roster, rocked the show and took bronze. I'd won the all-around by almost four points, yet I knew it hadn't been my greatest performance. For me, victory is more than just earning the highest score; it's also about doing my very best—and I wanted to do better. The question was: With the Summer Games right around the corner, would our Team USA hopefuls be able to peak at the exact right time?

Curiously, my Olympic dream had never been about winning—it was about *going*. It was about doing well enough at the Olympic trials to have my name called as a member of the team. It was about traveling to Rio with all the other American athletes and experiencing the excitement of the Olympic Village. It was about proudly wearing my country's colors on my chest and being excellent in the moments when it counted. It was about precision, confidence, and team-work. And it was about hope.

Then again, maybe turning my Olympic dream into a reality could be as simple as the advice my friend and team-mate Aly Raisman gave me at Nationals Camp that spring. We'd been roommates that week, and one day after practice, we were in our cabin slathering on facial masks and chasing away stress with our own impromptu spa day. At one point, I tore open a bag of Jolly Ranchers I'd brought with me and popped a piece of green apple hard candy into my mouth.

Aly snatched the bag away from me. "Simone, that's the last thing you need," she scolded me. "You never sleep any-way, and now you're going to get yourself all sugared up. I can just see you jumping up and down on the beds like a little kid who needs a nap but won't stay still long enough to go to sleep."

"Okay, Grandma Aly," I teased, because that's what we called Aly. At twenty-two, she was older than the other girls, and we all looked up to her. Before meets, she'd gather us around and remind us that we were in this together. Grandma Aly was also famous for passing out in her room after especially grueling practices. That girl loved a nap.

"Call me Grandma Aly all you want," she said now, not at all offended. "It's normal to want to sleep after a hard work-out. What's not normal is that you never nap, Simone. Who on earth has so much energy?"

I giggled when she said that, because ever since I was little, people had been telling me some version of exactly that. A decade and a half later, I was still that hyper, bouncing girl that my mom had enrolled in gymnastics classes so I'd have a place to burn off all that excess energy. These days, I thought of that energy as my own special superpower. It had allowed me to fall in love with flying. And it had taken me on an extraordinary journey that in a few short weeks might lead to me going to Rio.

As Aly and I spread thick cold cream on our faces, we talked about what the Olympic experience might be like this time around.

"You've won two Olympic gold medals," I said, meeting Aly's eyes in the mirror. "What's your best tip for doing well in Rio?

"Go to bed early," Aly shot back.

"What else?" I pressed.

"Remember to breathe," she said.

"And what else?"

Aly must have heard something in my tone that told her I was being serious, that I really wanted to know what she thought. She stopped spreading cream on her face and turned to look at me directly.

"Here's the thing you have to remember," she said. "The Olympics are just another World Championship event, so go out there and do exactly what you always do in practice. Just do exactly what you've already done three times at Worlds. It's really no different."

She dipped her fingers into the jar of cream, turned back to the mirror, and then paused. "Oh, and one more thing," she added. "Just don't look up at the Olympic rings."

CHAPTER 19

─────●─────

The Final Five

*"The fight is won or lost far away from
witnesses—behind the lines, in the
gym, and out there on the road, long
before I dance under those lights."*

—MUHAMMAD ALI, OLYMPIC AND PROFESSIONAL BOXER, ACTIVIST

I kept messing up on bars. I was over-rotating my hand-
stands, my catch-and-release moves were shaky, and the
timing was off on my whole routine. In two days, I'd join
the other four members of the US women's Olympic team at
the Karolyi Ranch to prepare for Rio, but at that moment, I
didn't look anything like an Olympic hopeful.

Hard to believe that only one week before, I'd placed first

at Trials in San Jose, California. That night, Martha Karolyi had named me to the team along with defending all-around Olympic champion Gabby Douglas; reigning Olympic floor champion Aly Raisman; the World champion on uneven bars Madison Kocian; and Laurie Hernandez, who'd edged into second place at Trials. I had been so proud of all of us in San Jose that night. As red, white, and blue confetti rained down on us and fog machines swirled clouds of vapor around us, we'd hugged each other, sobbing and laughing. I'd been on top of the world.

And now I was melting down.

Back in the WCC gym, my whole bar rotation was going wrong. I knew it was because I was working out on a different set of bars than I was used to, but I had to get accustomed to the new system because we'd be competing on it in Rio. The Gymnova bars were springier and swung me faster than the bar setup I'd trained on for most of my life—and that day, I just couldn't seem to get the hang of them. From our team group text, I knew some of the other girls were having as much trouble with the new bars as I was, but that didn't comfort me one bit. I wanted us all to succeed in Rio. Yet there I was, having visions of crashing to the mat in front of the entire world. What a disappointment I'd turn out to be.

Aimee saw me flinging myself around the bar and, just by looking at my movements, she could tell I was frustrated. She walked over to me. "Go home, Simone," she said. "That's enough for today. See you tomorrow."

I didn't argue. I just grabbed my grip bag, pulled on my black track pants, and strode out of the gym to my car. I sniffled the whole way home, fighting back feelings of failure. Once inside my room, I threw myself across the bed and really let myself bawl. My chest heaved, and I could barely catch my breath. I felt as if I was having a full-blown panic attack.

My dad came to see what all the commotion was about. The truth was, I'd been a little grumpy with my family ever since getting back from San Jose. The stress of having to follow up on my first-place finish at Trials was getting to me. Everywhere I looked, articles in magazines, newspapers, and online were declaring me America's best hope to win five gold medals in Rio. I refused to read any of the stories. How could I think about winning gold and making history when I couldn't even get my bar routine straight?

"Everything okay in here?" my dad asked from the doorway of my room. When I didn't answer, he walked over and put his hand on my shoulder. "Remember, you sometimes get like this before a big meet, Simone," he told me. "It will pass. It always does."

I buried my face in my pillow, seriously doubting that the pressure I was feeling would ever go away. My breath came in short gasps as I tried to control the crying.

"Do you want me to call Mr. Andrews?" Dad asked.

I nodded without saying a word, grateful to my father for knowing just what I needed in that moment.

A few minutes later, Dad brought the house phone to me. My sports psychologist was on the other end of the line. I hadn't talked to Mr. Andrews in several months because my schedule had been chock-full of workouts and competitions, sponsorship appearances and media interviews. Now, hearing Mr. Andrews' steady voice coming through the phone, I broke down again.

"Go ahead and cry," he said gently. "You probably need a good cry right now." And then he just waited, listening to me sob. A little while later, when I had finally cried myself out, he asked, "So what's worrying you, Simone?"

My big fear came tumbling out. "I don't think I'm going to be ready," I told him. "Everybody has all these huge expectations of me, and I'm afraid I won't be able to meet them."

"Well, you can't really worry about other people's expectations," he said. "You don't usually do that, so don't start worrying about that now. All you can truly control is committing yourself to practices and doing your best out there."

We talked about that a bit more, and then I thanked him. "I know how hard I've worked for this," I told him. "I think I'll be fine now." When I put down the phone, I really did believe that. Okay, Simone, just do what you know how to do. That's what I kept telling myself, and the next day at the gym, the extra bounciness of the new bars didn't seem like such a huge deal after all. In fact, I was starting to think that maybe I could use the springiness to help me fly even higher.

I sat on the floor of my bedroom, a suitcase open in front of me. I was trying to figure out how many leos I'd need for ten days of Olympic training camp. My teammates and I were all texting each other about what to pack. We finally decided that a dozen leos should be more than enough, and besides, the ranch had laundry facilities.

Once we solved the leotard dilemma, the conversation

turned back to the topic that had dominated our group text ever since Martha came into the holding room backstage after Trials and told us who would be going to Rio: We had to pick a group name. We passed over names like GLAM Squad—using the first initials for Gabby, Laurie, Aly, Maddie, Simone—because we wanted a name that wasn't just cute or clever, but also meaningful. Besides, GLAM Squad didn't include the initials of our alternates—Ashton Locklear, MyKayla Skinner, and Ragan Smith—who would be attending training camp and traveling to Brazil with us; they were as much a part of the team as we were.

Still, only five of us would ultimately compete in Rio, and our team name needed to reflect that. We finally settled on the Final Five. One reason was that we'd be the last five-member USA gymnastics team to go to the Olympics; starting with the 2020 Games in Tokyo, each country would send only four artistic gymnasts. But the main reason we chose our name was to pay tribute to Martha Karolyi. She'd be retiring at the end of the season, which meant the five of us would be the last team she mentored in her legendary career. We all agreed that we wouldn't reveal our name to Martha or anyone until after the team final. We aimed to take home gold, and we thought "the Final Five" would sound better if we had already won the biggest medal of our careers. It would be our way of thanking Martha for pushing each of us to be better than we ever believed we could be.

We all knew that the ten-day training camp we were about to attend would be beyond hard. "This just might be the toughest two weeks of my life," I said to Aimee the next day. We were in her car, driving down the long, narrow, wooded road that led to the ranch. Aimee had been selected as the official coach of the USA women's Olympic team the week before, which meant she'd be out on the floor with us in Rio and very involved in camp. But at the moment, as the familiar trees of the ranch brushed past her car windows, I was a little scared, if you want to know the truth. Five days at the ranch usually wore me out, and now we were facing ten days straight, after which we'd fly directly to Brazil without going back home.

"Aimee, we're all going to die!" I joked as the training center came into view. I clutched my throat for dramatic effect. "Save us, please!"

"Yes, you will die," my coach agreed, laughing. "And all of your hair will fall out too."

Aimee and I were keeping things light, and I was glad that I'd get to see my family one more time before heading off to Rio. There would be an open house at the ranch a few days before we departed for Brazil. Our families were all invited to visit us in Huntsville to see how our training was going, and we'd have a chance to say our good-byes then.

———

Mom has always believed in setting clear goals. When she, my dad, and my sister Adria arrived at the ranch for the family open house the following week, she took me aside to discuss the fact that I still hadn't written down any goals for my time in Rio.

"You said you wanted to make the team," she pointed out, "but now that you've made it, you need to set a new goal for what comes next. You need to write it down and be very purposeful about it."

"Mom," I protested, "not now. I don't want to think about that yet."

"But the Olympics are almost here," she said. "If you don't think about it now, when will you have time? You have to get clear on what you want to accomplish in Rio before you get there."

I put my arms around my mom, rested my forehead against hers, and groaned. All this talk of writing down goals was making me anxious. I still had several days of camp ahead of me, then another two weeks of practices in Brazil before podium training and the qualifying round.

"Just promise me this," Mom finally said. "Promise that you'll do your best. This is your dream, Simone, so go out there and live it with everything you've got. And don't forget to have fun."

I nodded, and we didn't say anything more about goals for the rest of the day. I guess Mom decided to let me handle the mental preparation on my own. But after my family left the ranch that evening, I couldn't stop thinking about what she'd said about me living my dream. For the rest of that week, in the back of my mind I was reflecting on what my true goals might be for my Olympic experience. Finally, on the day before our scheduled flight to Rio, I sat down in my cabin at the ranch, opened a notebook, and wrote my parents a short letter. We would all be sending our dirty clothes home in the suitcases we'd brought to camp, and we'd fold our sparkly new, custom-made red, white, and blue competition leos into two fresh suitcases provided by team sponsors. I planned to pack my notebook in the suitcase I was sending home, and I texted my sister Adria to ask her to make sure that Mom removed the notebook from the dirty laundry and read what I'd written. It was simply this:

Hi Mom and Dad,

I love you all.
See you soon in Rio.
I will make you proud.

Love, Simone. Kisses.

Mom told me later that when she read the words I will make you proud scrawled in my big, round handwriting in a notebook tucked between sweaty leos, she put her hand over her mouth and wept. She felt as if her prayers for me were being answered.

———

Our plane departed Houston on Tuesday night, July 26, 2016, at nine p.m. The eight of us tried to settle ourselves as passengers moving through the cabin stopped to take selfies with us. Ever since the Olympic Trials, people had started to recognize us. We were exhilarated to finally be on our way to Rio, but the long days of training had left us exhausted too. Once the plane door closed and the wheels lifted off the ground, we pulled blankets up to our chins and fell soundly asleep. I was knocked out right until the plane touched down in Brazil ten hours later. Then everything started moving at warp speed.

We got our credentials for the Olympic Village at the airport and took lots of press photos with the Rio mascot. Then we piled into a bus along with our coaches and trainers and drove almost an hour to the compound where the athletes would stay. We saw the tall buildings in the distance before we got to them, long rows of huge white apartment towers against a brilliant blue sky. At the gate, people came to help us with our bags and check us in at the Welcome Center. That's when we learned that Ashton, MyKayla, and Ragan would be staying at another compound, with all the other team alternates. We hugged them quickly and said good-bye. After that, we saw them only when they came to watch us compete and cheer us on.

The Olympic Village was like an athlete's fantasyland, with a pool and workout studios and a huge twenty-four-hour cafeteria with every style of food imaginable. There were Japanese, Brazilian, and Italian stations, as well as more Americanized choices such as pizza and burgers and pies, and healthier options, such as steamed chicken and fish with vegetables, or fruit and oatmeal—the kinds of foods we all knew we were supposed to eat, at least until the competition was over. I'd have to wait until I was back home to bite into a pizza slice.

The cafeteria is where we mingled with most of the other athletes, like Tom Daley, the British diver, and gymnast Arthur Nory Mariano, who I knew from international meets, and who the press kept calling my Brazilian boyfriend, even though we were just good friends. We also got to meet Simone Manuel, Michael Phelps, and Katie Ledecky from the US swimming team, and Novak Djokovic, the Serbian tennis player currently ranked number one in the world. We tried not to be too awestruck by all these stars, but one day a really tall, lean, muscular, dark-skinned man walked past our table with a small entourage. Aly and Gabby just about lost their minds.

"That's Usain Bolt!" they screamed. "Get your phone, let's take a picture!"

They jumped up so fast to get to him that they practically knocked our plates off the table, but one of the people with the Jamaican sprinter stopped them. "Not now," he said. "He's eating dinner." Later, when we'd finished our own meal, we all walked by Usain's table and apologized for disturbing him earlier, and he was super nice.

"We're the gymnastics team," we told him.

"I can tell," he said, with a big smile. Everyone knew who we were because we were so much shorter than the other athletes. I felt like an ant trying to make sure I didn't get stepped on.

Our apartment was in the American building; there were so many teams from the United States that we had an entire tower to ourselves. Our suite was on the third floor. When we walked in the first day, the whole space looked plain and a little unfinished. All the walls were white, the floor tiles were white, and in the living room were four green bean-bag chairs, three standing fans, and nothing else. There were four bedrooms off of the living room, each of them with two twin beds and a dresser. Aly and Maddie were in one room, Laurie and I were in another room, and Gabby had a room to herself. Our trainer was in the fourth room. We mostly lived out of our suitcases because the dressers were tiny. And there were no mirrors anywhere, not in the bedrooms or even in the bathroom. So the next day, our coaches brought in five standing mirrors.

Outside the living room was a balcony that overlooked the pool area. We had some of our best times in Rio on that balcony. We'd just sit there, worn out after practice, talking and chilling in our beanbag chairs with our feet up on the railing. Sometimes we'd be glued to our phones, scrolling through our Twitter feeds, laughing at a video someone had shared, or posting stories on Snapchat and Instagram. Other times, we'd watch Modern Family on Netflix on my computer, or dance to music that Laurie would blast from her playlist. We even posted a video of us singing along to Jake Miller's "Overnight." That was our jam.

From the balcony, we could watch the athletes from all over the world coming and going to the surrounding buildings, jogging along the footpaths, or doing laps in the pool. Everyone in the Olympic Village was constantly exercising, because we all had to be in the best shape of our lives. Martha made sure that none of us slacked off for even a single day. In fact, about an hour after we moved in on the first day, we were back on the bus, riding to the gymnastics training hall for our first workout in Rio.

Our daily regimen was just like at the ranch: workouts

twice a day on all four apparatuses, with a lunch break and some downtime in between. We were all eager to start competition. We'd practiced and practiced for weeks, and now we wanted to get out there and show everyone what we could do. I remember when I walked out with the team for the qualification round, I heard my mom's voice yelling, "Go, Simone!" I looked around the arena and found my family sitting over by the uneven bars. Once I located them in the crowd, even though I'd been slightly nervous before, I calmed right down. My mother, on the other hand, had been a bundle of jitters the night before while we were talking about the preliminaries on FaceTime. I had been the calm one then. "Mom," I said, "Don't worry about me. I'm ready."

And I was.

We all did well in the qualifying round, with me, Aly, and Gabby placing first, second, and third overall. The fact was, our whole team was so rigorously prepared that any one of us could have competed in the all-around. Unfortunately, the Olympic rules state that only the top two qualifiers from any country are permitted to participate. I understand and respect the rules, but for our team, it was still kind of a bummer. Despite this, we were all so enthralled just to be at the Olympics. One of my favorite memories of the qualification round came during our first rotation, which was the floor exercise. Laurie went before me, and after she finished her routine, I walked over to her. "Hey, Laurie," I said, "guess what? You're now officially an Olympian."

My roomie's face lit up with a huge grin. And after my floor routine, when I came down off the stage, she came over and high-fived me, still smiling. "Hey, Simone," she said, "guess what? You are now officially an Olympian."

Two days later, on Tuesday, August 9, our team did exactly what we had been training for so many years to do: We performed almost flawless routines and won team gold. If the all-around win was considered to be the jewel in the crown, the team medal was the crown itself—the main reason we were there. On the podium afterward, feeling the heavy gold disc around my neck, I felt so privileged to be standing with my teammates. All I could think was, Wow, we did it. How long have I dreamed about this? We were so happy for each other and for ourselves, but our job was only half over. The all-around competition and the event finals were still to come. I wasn't anywhere near finished trying to make my family and my country proud.

That afternoon, we told Martha that we'd named ourselves the Final Five as a tribute to her. When we explained how we'd all agreed on the name, she dabbed the corners of her eyes and said in her thick accent, "Oh my God, I love you guys even more now!" And she hugged us tightly. The rest of the afternoon and evening was a whirl of press interviews and photo ops, and then it was home to our little pod in the Olympic Village. We all fell right into bed, because we had to be up for our regular eight a.m. training the next morning. Before going to sleep, I carefully folded the green multicolored ribbon around my medal and put it at the bottom of my backpack. Later, they would give us sleek wooden cases to hold our medals, but for now, my makeshift storage would have to do.

"Can you believe we actually did it?" Laurie whispered, stifling a yawn before we drifted off. "We're not just Olympians now; we're gold medalists."

I was too exhausted from happiness to answer, so I just smiled. But when I awoke the next morning, I wasn't quite sure if the day before had all been a dream. I reached for my backpack and pulled out the medal, just to be sure. I unrolled the green ribbon and placed the gold disc in the palm of my hand, feeling its distinctive weight as I sent up a silent prayer of gratitude.

Thursday morning, the day of the Olympic all-around competition, dawned bright and clear. The apartment was silent when I opened my eyes. The rest of the girls except for Aly had already gone to breakfast. From there they would head to the training hall. Later, they would be in the gymnastics arena to see Aly and me battle it out with the best in the world for the coveted all-around title.

I went to find Aly. She was in her room and still in bed.

"I feel so good about today," I told her.

"Me too," she said, holding up one hand for a fist bump. "We're so prepared. I have a really good feeling."

My heart was galloping in my chest, but it wasn't nerves; it was excitement. I could hardly wait to get into the arena. Aly and I each showered and then we did our hair and makeup together in the living room. We took our time because the competition wouldn't begin until the early afternoon. I outlined my eyes in gold glitter and chose a nude lipstick instead of a bold one. The eye makeup, with my usual winged corners, was dramatic enough, and my sparkly leo would complete the effect. The night before, we'd chosen the leos we wanted to wear and laid them out on our beanbag chairs. Aly had opted for the shiny red with lines of crystals fanning out from the neckline like bursts of sunlight, while I'd selected a superpatriotic number with sheer white crystal-studded sleeves, and dazzling red-and-white stripes running from the shoulders down both sides, framing a high-sheen blue fabric dotted with glittering stars. I'd saved this leotard, my favorite, for the all-around. I hoped its shimmer would help me win gold.

I was already feeling incredibly happy to be sharing this day with Aly, who was such a rock-solid competitor and friend. As we walked to the bus that would take us to the arena, we held hands like schoolgirls and bobbed our heads to the music coming through our headphones. Every so often we'd hug each other and say, "You're good. You've worked so hard. You deserve to be here. You've got this." And then we'd say, "I love you so much. I love you, no matter what. Today will be a good day."

Our warm-up in the training hall went without a hitch or a fall, and then it was showtime. Before we walked out to compete, we always used the bathroom just in case. As I washed my hands and stared at my face in the mirror, my stomach was suddenly doing somersaults. I plopped down on a bench that was just outside the bathroom and tried to pull myself together. A few moments later, Aly walked out and sat down beside me. When she leaned her head back against the wall, I noticed she looked really pale.

"Are you okay?" I said.

She shook her head from left to right.

"Are you okay?" she asked me.

"No," I said. "I feel like I'm going to throw up."

The two of us sat there for several minutes, breathing slowly and trying to settle ourselves down.

"We're okay," I said after a while.

"We've got this," Aly said.

"We can do this."

"We've done this so many times."

"I love you, Aly."

"I love you, Simone."

"Let's go."

We did another fist bump and walked out onto the arena floor. Both Aly and I were in the same group as the top contenders from Russia, China, and Brazil. As the announcer introduced us to the audience, we stepped forward and waved. Then, as I'd done in every meet ever since I was a pint-sized JO competitor, I listened for my mother's voice. "You've got this, Simone!" she called from somewhere over by the uneven bars. Her words were almost drowned out by the rest of my family members, who were screaming just as loudly. In fact, the whole auditorium was going crazy, which was a good thing. It's way more nerve-wracking for gymnasts to perform our death-defying routines against a backdrop of silence. I loved the roar of a fully engaged audience, and the crowd in Brazil was one of the best.

Our first rotation was vault. By the time I stepped onto the mat, my queasiness had subsided. Okay, Simone, just like practice, I thought, remembering the mantra Kyla Ross had given me at my first major assignment three years before. At the flag, I smiled and saluted the judges, adjusted my starting position, and took off sprinting down the runway. I could feel that my form was nearly perfect as I pushed off the vault table. I spun twice around in the air, my body fully extended, and added another half twist before landing. But so much adrenaline was pumping through me that I needed a step to balance myself as my feet touched the mat. I'd known as soon as I punched off the vault that I was soaring too far out and wasn't going to stick the landing. I was annoyed with myself as I stepped off the mat to meet Aimee. She wasn't worried.

"It was a good Amanar," she assured me. She slipped an arm around my shoulders as we squinted up at the Jumbotron, waiting for the score. It turned out that I'd executed well enough to earn a score of 15.866, which put me in first place, about a point ahead of Aly, who'd also performed a strong Amanar.

Next up: the uneven bars. As I walked up to the low bar, getting ready to mount and swing myself up to the high bar, I was sure I heard my mother's distinctive Belizean accent: "Make it count, Simone!" A moment later, I was flying higher on my Tkatchev than I ever had. I caught the high bar firmly on my way back around and glided seamlessly into the Pak salto. Every skill flowed effortlessly into the next one, and I stuck the dismount as if my feet were glued to the mat. I was smiling as I came down from the apparatus, confident that I'd delivered.

But it wasn't enough. My score, 14.966, was lower than I'd hoped, probably because my start value on bars wasn't as high as on my other routines.

"Shake it off," Aimee told me, because as far as she was concerned, I'd done one of my best bar routines ever.

Martha agreed with her. "The score doesn't show it," Martha said, winking at me, "but we know it."

Still, my lower-than-expected score opened the door for Russia's Aliya Mustafina to move into first place. Not once since my first Worlds win in 2013 had any competitor's name been above mine in an all-around meet. Everyone seemed shocked by this turn of events, but I wasn't really surprised. Aliya is a top-caliber bar specialist, and she'd tied with Maddie Kocian for the bars title at the last Worlds. And that afternoon, she had been spectacular on bars, which had earned a huge score for her. I took a deep breath and reminded myself that I still had beam and floor to come, and my start values for both those routines were higher than anyone else's, with Aly's close behind. Of course, high start values would mean nothing if my execution wasn't on point. Every skill had to be flawless.

I was first up on beam in the third rotation. When I completed the two and a half circles of my wolf turn cleanly, I knew I was in the zone. I was connecting all my skills smoothly, with no hesitation between moves. I felt confident, especially when I caught sight of Martha on the sidelines, smiling broadly. Okay, just the dismount left, I thought as I positioned my feet against the chalk mark I'd made on the beam earlier. Mine was the one with the S drawn through it, so there would be no confusion about where to start my final double-twisting double tuck, the hardest dismount in the world. As I was twirling through air, I already knew I was going to stick the landing—bam!

The whole arena erupted in wild applause as I lifted my chest and raised my arms high. Relief flooded through me as it always does once my beam set is over. I jumped down from the mat and into Aimee's arms. I tried not to stress as I waited for the score. I knew I'd done everything I could up there, and now it was up to the judges. Suddenly, the audience broke into a fresh round of cheers. I looked up and saw the verdict: 15.433. I'd retaken the lead.

Now only one event was left—the one in which I was the most confident. I'd always loved the excitement and drama of tumbling on floor. But as naturally as the skills came to me, this was the Olympics, and I didn't want to take anything for granted. I mean, what if I tripped going into a leap or something silly like that? What if I took off with too much power and stepped out of bounds? All of this was going through my head as I walked onto the floor. I was the last gymnast to perform, and though I didn't know it at the time, I only needed 13.833 to win. I could have fallen once, even twice, and still made that score, but I wanted to do my very best. If I took home gold, I didn't want anyone to doubt that I deserved it, so I needed to go out there and earn it. And that's what I did. As my samba music filled the arena, the crowd began to clap in time with the beat. Energized,

I flipped and somersaulted, taking in the whole thrilling 360-degree view of the arena from high in the air. As I came down on the mat on my final tumbling pass, I think I was the happiest athlete in Rio. And when my score appeared, it was the highest of the competition—15.933. I had done it! Gold!

Aly was right behind me with the silver, and Aliya Mustafina had taken the bronze. Aly, Aimee, and I hugged each other ecstatically, tears of joy spilling out from our lower lids. Then Aly pushed me in the direction of the stage. "Go! Go!" she said, "Get up there!" In a daze, I went back out on the floor, waving at the applauding crowd. But it didn't feel right being up there without Aly, so I motioned for her to come up on stage with me. We had done the whole competition together, and now we would finish it together, joining our hands and lifting them high in a victory salute to the crowd. "We're basically like sisters," Aly told me that night. "We'll have this moment forever."

Much later, I found out that as soon as the all-around rankings appeared on the Jumbotron, television cameras zoomed in on my mother and sister up in the stands, sobbing their hearts out. The cameras lingered on my family as my father wrapped his arms around my mom, kissed her on the lips, and rested his head on hers. What the cameras didn't show was that behind his glasses, my father's eyes were glistening too.

Each day of our competition in Rio went much the same way. Our team hardly made a mistake. And when all the contests had been held, all the events finals completed, I had earned two more gold medals for vault and floor, and a bronze on beam. Laurie turned in an impressive performance to take silver on beam—I was so proud of my roommate. Aly had also won silver on floor, and Maddie had taken silver on bars, making us the most decorated American Olympic gymnastics team. My win on vault in particular meant a lot to me. I'd never earned gold on vault in a world competition—until now. I learned afterward that I'd made history by becoming the first American woman ever to win gold in that event at the Olympics.

My beam performance in the event final wasn't quite as golden: I'd bobbled on my front tuck and would have fallen all the way off the beam if I hadn't grabbed it with both hands. That knocked my score down by a full point. I was sure that put me out of medal contention, but it turned out that my execution on the rest of the routine, combined with the high level of difficulty, was enough to push me into third place. Most commentators assumed that getting bronze on beam would devastate me, but in fact, I was over the moon. Of course, I wished I'd been able to get through the entire routine without a mistake, but who falls on beam at the Olympics and still wins a medal? It's rare. Standing next to Laurie and first-place winner Sanne Wevers of the Netherlands during the medal ceremony, I was grinning every bit as hard as if I'd just won gold.

On my last day of competition, when I went out to perform my routine for the floor exercise final, the audience was cheering and shouting wildly for me. The racket was insane. I felt so thankful to every person in that arena for the way they'd supported all the gymnasts throughout the Games.

The Brazilians were easily the most generous audience we've ever had, and their enthusiasm meant even more to us because we were not in our own country, yet they cheered for us like we were the home team. That loud audience was part of the reason I was feeling a little sad after my floor routine. When the announcer called my name and the official placed the medal around my neck, it was bittersweet. At first, I had felt a rush of relief that everything had gone even better than I'd dared hope. I'd nailed every tumbling pass, spinning high in the air. And I'd stuck all my landings, capping off my Olympic experience with yet another gold. But I'd been waiting my entire life for a chance to go to the Olympics, and just like that, the experience was already behind me. I remember thinking, I'm a little bit tired now, and I could feel the stress melting away. But underneath it all, I felt a little tinge of sorrow, because I realized that everything I'd just experienced was now over.

Our team moved out of the Olympic Village a couple of days later and checked into the Grand Hyatt hotel. Most of my extended family had already left Rio, but my parents and Adria were still there. I couldn't wait to see them, but I only got to hug and catch up with them for a half hour, because the team had a schedule packed with press interviews, TV appearances, and photo shoots. Aly, Maddie, and I did go to the beach for a few hours, and that was fun, but mostly we were caught up in a media whirlwind.

Not that I'm complaining, because in the middle of that whirlwind, another impossible dream of mine actually came true. Everyone who knows me knows about my crazy crush on the twenty-nine-year-old actor Zac Efron. I even had a life-sized cardboard cutout of him back home in Texas. I loved his movies, but mostly, I thought he was cute, and I'd heard that he's really a good person. Well, right after my event final in floor, my teammates and I were scheduled to do a taping for the TODAY Show. We'd gotten to know one of the hosts, Hoda Kotb, when she interviewed us after the team final, and she was a lot of fun. She knew all about my crush on Zac Efron, and she'd even threatened to bring him to Rio.

"I'm going to need a defibrillator," I'd joked, because of course, I thought she was just teasing me. Little did we know that her producers had flown Zac to Rio after the floor exercise final to surprise us. When he walked out on set wearing a navy blue USA sweatshirt and green khaki shorts, I thought I was going to pass out. Seriously. We all started screaming, and Laurie went to hug him right away. I actually ducked behind Aly, hiding because I suddenly felt so shy.

Zac was as warm and welcoming as I'd always heard that he was. "Hey, I'm the one with the butterflies," he said as he hugged us one by one. Then, when I finally came out from behind Aly, he lifted me right up onto his hip and planted a big kiss on my cheek. I almost died. I was giggling so hard,

all I could think was, This can't be real life. This is too perfect to be real. Zac Efron was even more gorgeous in person
and way nicer than I imagined. He told us, "When I found
out you guys were fans, I was like, what am I doing sitting
here on the couch? I have to come see you. I have to come
hang out and support you guys, because you're America's
true heroes right now."

As if meeting Zac Efron wasn't enough, I'd also received
supportive messages from Kim Kardashian, Jake Miller,
Samuel L. Jackson, Taylor Swift, and even Hillary Clinton.
And after I led the American delegation into the Maracanã
Stadium for the closing ceremony, President Barack Obama
and Mrs. Obama also tweeted me:

> Couldn't be prouder of #TeamUSA. Your determina-
> tion and passion inspired so many of us. You carried
> that flag high tonight, @Simone_Biles!

Someone said later, "Simone Biles is having the best week
of her entire life." I don't know who said that, but with Zac
Efron and President and Mrs. Obama and so many others
congratulating us on our team's Olympic victories, I'd have
to say that statement was entirely true.

No one was more surprised than I was when my agent
gave me the news that Team USA—all the athletes in all
the sports we'd competed in over the past seventeen days—
had voted for me to carry the American flag at the closing
ceremony. I hadn't even known I was in the running. Me!
All four-foot-eight-inches of me had been chosen to carry
a nine-foot-tall flag! I didn't know whether to be thrilled

or terrified. Michael Phelps had carried the flag during the opening ceremony, but he was so much taller than I was. I knew I was strong, but that flag had looked ginormous and hard to hold. Would I be able to manage it? I knew that being selected by my peers for this final Olympic assignment was the highest honor, but I was secretly worried that I'd embarrass my country.

I was relieved that the flagpole wasn't as heavy as it looked, and I carried it easily, despite the fact that the night was windy and rainy. The Americans created gridlock at the entrance to Maracanã Stadium, as one athlete after another bent to take selfies with me holding that giant flag. Finally, our delegation paraded onto the field with me leading the way, a small figure in white shorts and white shirt, barely visible under the huge banner of our country. At some point during the ceremony, a feeling of peace settled over me. I had represented my country well. I had not wasted the talents and opportunities God gave me, and I'd tried to be, as my mom put it, the best Simone I could be.

That night as I held the American flag steady, I saw that everything I had been through, all the sacrifices my family and I had made to get to this moment, had been worth it. I wouldn't have changed any of it. Even if things hadn't gone my way, I still wouldn't have wished that a single moment would be different. Every challenge I'd ever faced had made me stronger and more determined. When I'd failed to make the national team five years before, it had forced me to commit myself to becoming a better gymnast. And as hard as it had been to give up my dream of attending my high school prom with my friends, the decision to be homeschooled had freed me to embrace an even greater possibility—of one day standing on an Olympic gold medal podium with my teammates. Who knew that the tiny girl with the big muscles jumping on a backyard trampoline would one day hold an American flag twice her size on a rainy night in Rio while the whole world looked on?

I could hardly wait to see where my life would take me next, what new goals I would set for myself, what dreams I would hold on to. But all of that was still to come. Now, in the carnival-like atmosphere of the Maracanã Stadium, marching with athletes from all over the globe, I knew that somewhere high up in the stands my parents and my sister were sharing this moment with me. As incredible as my Olympic journey had been, my greatest gift had been the chance to bring joy to those who love me most—my family. More than all of the gold medals in the world, I'd wanted to make them proud. After all, it was Mom and Dad who'd first given me the courage to dream such a big dream and to soar higher than I'd ever imagined I could. They'd known all along that I had wings. They'd just been waiting for me to spread them.

ACKNOWLEDGMENTS

I didn't make it all the way to Rio on my own; my family, friends, and loved ones have taken this journey with me. I'm very grateful to have the world's greatest cheering section in my life, and each one has had a part in helping me strive for my dreams. So many people have given me their love and encouragement, and here are just a few that I'd like to thank publicly:

My parents: Thank you, Mom and Dad, for putting up with me on a daily basis. I know it isn't easy! And thank you for sacrificing so much of your time for me to do what I love. Without you, I wouldn't be who I am today. I love you both more than you can imagine.

Adria, oh, Adria, where to start: Thank you for being the craziest—and for always making me laugh when I don't want to smile. I love you, sister.

Ron and Adam: Thank you for always giving me the best life advice and for keeping my spirits high. You guys really are the best brothers; no one can compare. I love you guys!

Paul and Judy: Thank you for being the greatest godparents ever. I was truly blessed with the best. I love you both.

Aunt Corrine: Thank you for being the one I can go to when my mom says no. Kidding, but thank you for treating me like your third daughter (sorry, Corleigh and Alyssa!). You always have the best words of encouragement and advice, and you always bring the party no matter where we go, which I love!

Uncle Leighton: Thank you for creating the best video montages and sharing them at all the family gatherings.

Uncle Barnes: Thank you for all the good luck and congrats texts before and after all of my competitions. They're the best!

Aunt Margaret, Aunt Harriet, Aunt Jennifer, Uncle Silas, Uncle Warren, and every one of my relatives: I'm so thankful that I have such a big and loving family! You have made a difference in my life just by your encouragement and presence over the years.

Alyssa and Corleigh: I love you both. Thanks for being the most supportive, loving cousins I could ever ask for!

Coach Aimee: Thank you for molding me into the gymnast I always wanted to be and for never giving up on me. Without you, I wouldn't have accomplished my dreams. I love you.

Janey Miller, my agent at Octagon: I can't thank you enough for making my schedule and my life easier and, of course, for setting up the most amazing sponsors. I couldn't have asked for a better agent.

Farley Chase, my literary agent: Thank you for all of the behind-the-scenes work you did to make this book a reality.

Michelle Buford, my cowriter: Thank you for listening to my endless number of crazy stories and for transforming them into a beautiful inspiration for both kids and adults.

Father Charlie: Thank you for being a wonderful spiritual guide. I'm grateful to have you in my life.

Miss Heather and Miss Susan: Thank you for working with me one-on-one and for helping me do the best school-work possible so I could still train for the number of hours I needed to. And thank you for helping me get all the correct credits I needed to graduate.

Maggie Nichols: Thanks for dealing with my craziness at every national team camp and on every single US assignment we had together. You're the best roommate and best friend I've ever had.

Alec Yoder: Thanks for being there after almost every competition to hang out with my hungry, crazy, hyper self. I can't thank you enough for being one of my best friends who I can always go to for anything, in and out of the gym.

Caitlyn Cramer: Thank you for being there in the very beginning and for sticking by my side throughout this whole journey. You are the definition of a best friend.

Rachel Moore: Thank you for being my right hand, my go-to, and my un-biological sister. There are no right words to describe our crazy friendship. Love ya!!!

Robert Andrews: Thank you for allowing me to realize that a person isn't actually crazy just for seeing a sports psychologist! Also thank you for allowing me to push my mental willpower past the limits so I could fully believe in myself under any circumstances or pressure.

Dr. Rand: Thanks for helping to keep my body healthy and in one piece throughout this journey. I appreciate you and your whole team at Methodist Hospital and Rehab.

TEAM USA/USA Gymnastics: Thank you for allowing me to pursue my dreams and aspirations at the elite level.

And thank you for giving me the opportunities of a lifetime. There's no better team than Team USA!

Family, friends, and fans: Thank you for always believing in me during my entire journey to Rio. I love you all endlessly.

My book team: I really do appreciate the skill and hard work that everyone at Zondervan and HarperCollins put into my book. A special thanks to Zondervan's Senior Vice President Annette Bourland, who signed me up for the project and who has been enthusiastic about my story from day one. Also thanks to Andrea Vinley Jewell and Jacque Alberta for editing the manuscript. And much appreciation goes to Londa Alderink, vice president of marketing, as well as to the art director, photo editor, marketing team, and the incredible sales force.

CONNECT WITH
SIMONE BILES
ONLINE!

 /simonebiles

@simone_biles

simonebiles

Visit Simone's website at www.simonebiles.com